TIER SIX

Marci Giebels

Misty Morn Publishing

TIER SIX
Misty Morn Publishing

ISBN 978-0-578-14381-1

To my wise and beautiful children . . . *I love you "infinity"*

THE TRANSITION TIER

The Transition Tier was utopia for all--an ever-changing canvas that responded to each living thing that occupied the space. For some, it was an oceanside sunset. For others, it was a crowded city street where it was impossible to feel alone. The Tier was always moving, shifting, and molding. The young man stood straight and tall in the nothingness. For him, paradise wasn't the presence of anything, just the absence of his tormenting heartache.

His serene mood produced the fragrance of orange blossoms. It was his favorite scent because it reminded him of her, but the reminder wasn't comforting. The young man began to panic.

His thoughts were not private in the Transition Tier and support came quickly.

"Welcome, Journeyer." The Spirit's voice resonated like a thought. "Congratulations on passing Tier Five. Are you ready to proceed to Tier Six, or do you require more rest?"

The Spirit glowed brightly, but the illumination did not hurt the young man's newly reborn eyes, as it would have on Tier Five. Still, he squinted out of habit. He knew that the behaviors from his most recent lifetime would stay with him for a while.

The presence reassured the young man. He spoke softly, but deliberately, "You know what I'm going to ask for. You know me better than I know myself."

"My knowing will not lead you to Enlightenment. It is your knowing that matters," The Spirit answered gently.

"Right. Well, what I know is that my Plan was altered, which created consequences that I need your help to rectify. My Plan was decided, but now I'm on a whole different Path, which can't be right because I was on the right Path before. I just need help returning to it."

"Would you like to see your loved one? Would it be easier for you to move forward if you could witness her happiness? She is having a peaceful Journey on Tier Four."

"I can't be separated from her any longer. It's been two lifetimes." The young man's voice cracked with emotion.

"There is no measure of time. You are with those you love, in the now."

"Oh, yeah, right. Thanks for reminding me. That's super comforting." The young man reverted to sarcasm and found the slip to be satisfying.

"Would you like to view Tier Four?" The Spirit asked again patiently.

"No." The young man closed the eyes that he had come to think of as his own. He had retained this vessel since the lifetime when he met her. He knew that his physical appearance was irrelevant, but he hoped that the consistency might make him easier for her to recognize.

"Would you like to retain your memories of Tier Five? You are not rewarded or penalized for collecting memories and your soul will have the benefit of your experiences whether you are aware of those memories or not. You will graduate to higher frequencies, regardless of your awareness to do so."

The options were always the same. The Spirit recited them every time that you came through the Transition Tier. The young man had retained memories from his last three Journeys, so he knew the routine.

"Retain memories," he answered gruffly. The Spirit knew what he would do. Sometimes free will was redundant and slowed the process.

"Tier Six is even more lovely than Tier Five. There is much to absorb and much to be gained," The Spirit told him.

The young man opened his eyes and glanced apprehensively beneath his feet at the other Tiers, wondering which one would be his Tier Six. It was like looking through a skyscraper with glass floors. Numbered Tiers were worlds unto themselves, each containing lovingly planned challenges, unexpected rewards, and predestined connections with other beings. Life teemed in every dimension and on each frequency. All living things existed simultaneously in the present, unaware of the others on different planes.

She was somewhere in the intricate layers. He spent two lifetimes searching tirelessly for her, fueled by the belief that once two souls were joined, nothing could keep them apart. Knowing that she existed somewhere without him made the young man feel empty. Pain could not enter the Transition Tier, but the other side of love is always as close as love itself.

Not caring if he appeared immature, the young man tried one more time. "Why did you send her to me? It's torture to love her the way I do. Please let me stay here with you until she arrives. Allow us to continue together to the next Journey—the way it was supposed to be before . . . before she was taken."

"I know your desire, and I know what is most beneficial for you. "

The other side of love broke through and the young man was filled with fear. Agonizing fear that he would never find her. Fear that she would forget him. Fear of what he would become without her.

The Spirit responded with compassion. A satisfactory resolution could not be revealed at this time. The Spirit knew that the young man would be happier if he were actively engaged in the process that would eventually lead to his Enlightenment.

"There are very few Tiers left before you will transcend your being and progress to Knowing," The Spirit whispered gently. "Tier Six is where you belong. Increase your faith. I will give you all that you need. Go with love."

The young man was aware that the smell of orange blossoms was fading. He felt himself shifting from one dimension to another. There was a sense of being lifted. He arrived on Tier Six and, unwillingly, started over.

CHAPTER ONE
EIGHTEEN YEARS LATER

Mark didn't know if there was any science behind his philosophy, but starting the day with push-ups seemed to have a detoxifying effect on him. As he slowly executed each controlled repetition he felt his head clear as the endorphins tricked his body into thinking it felt good. Mark didn't know if the hormone ate up the alcohol that lingered in his bloodstream from the night before, but the oxygen he was adding to the mix seemed to help. The banging in his head got louder as his blood raced and he tried to obscure the sound by keeping track of his reps out loud. He was on the way to two hundred.

"Fifty-one, fifty-two . . ." Mark stopped in plank position, his body completely straight and tense, only his toes and the first two knuckles of each fist touched the floor. He was careful to stay centered, as a slight shift forward or back would mean hitting his head on one bulkhead or banging his heels into the other. His six-foot, four-inch frame made his living quarters a tricky fit.

"Shit." Mark moved faster than he thought possible and made it to the toilet before the violent heaves turned productive.

He flushed the contents of his stomach. "Shit." Mark whispered his favorite word one more time. He remembered the word from Tier Three where he had lived the most fulfilling lifetime in his memory and where he had connected with his soul mate.

If he hadn't been so young and physically strong, his body wouldn't have been able to withstand the punishment he put it through. He knew that he didn't have to worry too much about the effects the abuse would have on his vessel. It only had to last one lifetime before it would be completely regenerated in preparation for the next one.

He knew that if he looked in the mirror he would see that his blue eyes were bloodshot, his seditious five o'clock shadow had become an overgrown blond beard, and the color of his skin matched the gray walls of his undersized living quarters. So he didn't look in the mirror.

"Are you alive in there?" The voice came from a monitor mounted on the bulkhead in his stateroom. Mark glanced at the screen and saw an image that looked eerily like he did—on a good day. They say that when people spend a lot of time together they start to look alike. For Mark and Wentworth, the physical similarities went beyond that explanation, but the two had spent the last twelve years together at the orphanage on the Surface.

"Yup." Mark tried to fake some enthusiasm, but he couldn't even convince himself.

"The drink will kill you, you know. Eventually."

"With any luck."

"You're needed on the Bridge. The General has some questions for you about your recruitment papers. Your name change and stuff like that, okay?"

"Are you supposed to be telling me this, or was it supposed to be a surprise?" Mark skillfully avoided the camera attached to his monitor.

"This is an official wake-up call and an unofficial heads-up call. You've been written up three times this month. Once more and you're expelled. Just get up here. You have ten minutes." The screen went black.

Mark laughed at the thought of going to the Bridge as he was currently dressed, in his boxers. That would be one way to divert the General's attention from the questions he wanted to ask. Mark pressed the button next to his hanging locker and listened for the "pshhhhhh" that meant his charcoal slacks and his regulation military button-up were steaming. Mark figured that a perfect uniform would balance his otherwise disheveled appearance and there was only so much a guy could do in ten minutes when the walk would take six and a half. Mark dressed, ran a shine cloth over his shoes, and absent-mindedly finger combed his bald head.

Mark's quarters were among the rest of the trainees' on Deck Three. When he entered the passageway, it was already alive with go-getters competing for the proverbial worm.

"Mark, Dude, you gonna give me a chance to win back that twenty I lost to you last night?"

"Already spent it, Sanders, but I'll take another twenty from you whenever you want," Mark said with a friendly smile.

He fell in with crewmembers walking on the starboard side of the ship toward the bow. Mark threw lighthearted jabs at several oncoming trainees as he moved through the passageway. He had to greet his buddies with a left jab due to the traffic pattern, so the punches didn't land as solidly as they would have if the rules for foot traffic aboard the battleairship were reversed.

Mark moved slowly through the six-foot wide passageway due to the mandate that crewmembers walk single file. Ahead of him, a seemingly endless line of guys his age walked through the gray hallway on the gray floor and were dressed in the same gray uniform that he wore. The only variety in the landscape was the various colors of scalps that had been revealed when the recruits had been forced to shave their heads. Mark fantasized about sprinting down the center of the passageway and wondered what the punishment could be for doing it.

"There's something on your face, Mead," a trainee joked as Mark passed.

"Don't worry Mason, you'll grow whiskers once you hit puberty," Mark answered.

A lot of the guys in the passageway laughed as they proceeded in an orderly fashion.

Mark finally got to the stairs and climbed up two decks to emerge on the upper deck. He paused to look forward and aft. He was amidships of the 1,000-foot long battleairship, which was aloft at about 30,000 feet. The walkway to the Bridge was encased in glass and Mark could appreciate the bulk of the ship from his current vantage point. This was the newest battleairship of the World Army's twenty-ship fleet and it was a beauty. It had come online the year before in 2069. Mark knew that when he turned nineteen, he would be expected to move to full soldier status, but he had no intention of enlisting. Training gave him a free place to stay and lots of privileges, so he planned to enjoy the ride until it was over. Once he left the World Army, he would never see a view like this again.

Mark took a mental picture of the blue abyss and ran up the final set of stairs that led him to the Bridge and the General's office.

"Trainee Mead to see General Walthers," Mark announced to a young sergeant sitting behind a desk in the General's outer office.

"General Walthers is expecting you. Get in there."

Mark tried to execute the salute the Army soldiers had taught him many times, but it never turned out as sharp as the other guys'.

When Mark entered the office, the five-star General was behind his desk. The hologram of a soldier stood on his blotter and the General devoted his full attention to the computer-generated image. Mark stood at attention, waiting for the General to acknowledge him.

"That concludes the oh-eight-hundred update, General. Is there any other way I can be of service, Sir?" The voice came from the six-inch tall 3D image.

"No, Captain. That is all." General Walthers pressed a button and the hologram was gone. He looked up at Mark. "Sit."

Mark sat in the single chair on the other side of the General's massive desk.

"Do you understand that giving false information to the military is considered treason, which is an offense punishable by death?" the General's eyes seared into Mark. He paused for a fraction of a second, but before Mark could answer, the General continued.

"Keeping that in mind, for the official record, what is your name?"

His Tier Three name had been his favorite and, when he signed up for the pleasure cruise, he used it.

"Mark Mead, Sir," he replied.

"Death, Trainee. That is your last reminder. Mark Mead didn't exist until you accepted the rank of trainee with the World Army using that name."

"I'm not nineteen yet, Sir, and I don't have to register on the Surface or enlist until I am. I didn't know that what I did before age nineteen was important."

"You have a criminal record?" The General didn't blink. "Are you hiding? Your fingerprints didn't red-flag, but there are ways to manipulate digital files."

"No, Sir. My mother died when I was five and my father took me to the orphanage—"

"You mean the World Army sponsored school where you were educated and where you were given food, shelter, and clothing?" The General corrected him.

Mark cleared his throat. "Yes, Sir. When I graduated from The World Army School, the counselor advised me to go into training. I didn't want my family name because they were never really a family to me, so I changed it."

"There is a legal way to do that, you know." General Walthers leaned on his desk, closing the gap between himself and Mark. "You sure you want to be Mark Mead?" Mark assumed the General could read his thoughts.

"Yes, Sir."

The General smiled smugly, his eyes still locked on Mark's unaffected stare. He leaned back in his chair and pressed a button on his desktop. "If you want the Army to call you Mark Mead, you have to file an official name change." Another hologram appeared on the General's blotter.

"Yes, Sir."

"Get it done. I'm watching you, Mead. Don't piss on my Army, boy. When you enlist I will make you a god, but I can also make hell look appealing. You want to keep floating in my battleairship, above the shit?" Mark assumed this was a rhetorical question. "Then you better become a model trainee. And shave. Now. Dismissed."

The General turned his attention to the new hologram that had appeared between them and Mark stood up too fast, bringing a swirling sensation into his head. He tried to remain steady on his feet as he reached the door.

"Are you expelled?" The voice from his bedroom monitor rang in his ears again. This time it was live and walked the passageway directly in front of Mark.

"No, Wentworth, I am not expelled."

"Does he have a gas mask on? Because you reek of drink."

"He drinks so much, he's probably immune to the smell."

Wentworth lowered his voice as they walked through the heavily populated passageway of the battleairship. "You can get expelled for drinking, and for falsifying records."

"Where do you think I get the drink? We're hovering at thirty thousand feet on a battleairship—I'm getting it from the enlisted soldiers. Everybody drinks on this ship. Everyone but you, my rule-following, no-fun-having friend."

"Soldiers have the best lives possible and I'm not blowing my chance to become one. I'm not going to wind up on the Surface again worrying about disease, air quality, or how I'm going to eat. Look around you, Mark. This isn't just a thousand feet of gleaming steel. It's as much fresh food and purified water as you want, filters making sure there isn't a speck of dust contaminating the air, living quarters with your own bathroom, and freshly laundered sheets on your soft bed every night. The Army provides everything I need on this beautiful ship and I'm not gonna screw it up." Wentworth took two fast-paced and determined steps before reaching the slower moving trainee ahead of him in the single file line.

"You are a boring, cowardly man." Mark laughed good-naturedly, smiling at his friend's back. "Aren't you supposed to be puppy-dogging for the General right now?"

Wentworth let the gap between him and the person in front of him widen, "It's my squad's turn to go to the Surface to deliver supplies."

"A trip to the Surface?" Mark's face lit up. "Awesome."

"You say that because you don't have to go," Wentworth replied. "I spent so many years hoping to get away from there. I feel like every time I go back I'm tempting fate to trap me there again."

"Let me go in your place. I'd do anything for a few hours away from this hunk of gleaming steel." Mark patted his beard as if reverently comforting a dying pet. "I have to shave anyway. Come to my quarters; we'll switch ID's, just like old times. You can stay in my mouse hole until I get back."

Wentworth and Mead had learned to take advantage of their uncanny resemblance during their many years together at school. They had the same build, brother-like features, and their coloring was almost a perfect match. They had adequately mastered each other's mannerisms, allowing Wentworth to take just enough tests as Mead to keep his buddy enrolled. Mark's charisma made him very popular with the girls, so he set up a few dates for his buddy to repay the favor.

"I couldn't ask you to do that." Wentworth shook his head.

"Dude, you didn't ask me and I'm not asking you. You have nothing to say about it—the decision has been made." Mark shadowboxed and, with a knock-out blow, declared a victory for himself by strutting the rest of the way to his quarters with both fists raised above his head.

CHAPTER TWO

Echoes of what happened in the Transition Tier sometimes came back to Mark when he least expected it. He didn't have clear memories of everything that went on there, but he did remember being told that Tier Six was lovely.

As the shuttlecraft descended to the Surface, Mark looked through the porthole at the familiar setting. Russet colored, featureless landscape went on as far as you could see. The only contrast was from the fires. Sometimes a flare-up came from the core and people lit fires to clean up the messes they made. As the craft flew over a community of Dwellers, Mark studied their campsites. Some were sheltered by a piece of fabric suspended horizontally at ceiling height and others were open to the sky. Some Dwellers hung pieces of cloth to form walls between their camp and the neighbors'. All of the homes were open to the dust and in plain view of passersby. There were paths worn into the Surface grime that acted as roads and provided borders to the rows of dwellings.

Mark felt duped. Perhaps an evolution was in the works, but, at this point, the loveliness of this place escaped him.

When the Surface Dwellers heard the Army shuttlecraft, they came running. They knew that food and water were on board along with other necessary items. Mark was close enough above them to see the desperation in their eyes. No, there was nothing lovely about this place.

The craft landed a mile outside of the shantytown they had just flown over, and then transformed to a land vehicle. Treads kept the vehicle moving so that it was never vulnerable.

Mark and three other trainees removed their seatbelts and went aft to their assigned station in the cargo hold of the shuttlecraft. Their job was moving the pallets of twenty-pound bags down the rollers of the aft lift gate. The supplies sped up on the decent and landed on the Surface in a controlled crash. The delivery method was designed to be distant and impersonal.

A trainee who looked younger than Mark, was at least six inches shorter than Mark, and displayed more ambition to be the leader than Mark, took charge. "I'm Chapman, this is Brown." He pointed to the trainee standing beside him. "I've done a lot of these runs, so you guys can just follow my lead."

Mark rolled his eyes. He couldn't stand the rank and file BS that often happened when there was no superior present to control a situation. There were four hundred crewmembers on the battleairship and most of them were undistinguished. When a high-ranking soldier was not on site, everyone wanted to assume the role.

"You two, uh . . . what's your names?"

"Wentworth," Mark spoke in a voice a few octaves lower than his already booming baritone to unnerve Chapman and it worked. The young cadet blinked a few times in rapid succession as he sized Mark up.

The guy standing next to Mark shook his head, laughed under his breath and said something that Mark couldn't hear.

"You two roll the pallets down the lift gate and we'll get 'em lined up for you," Chapman directed.

"Why do we have to be closest the open cargo door?" The guy next to Mark asked.

"Dude, if they want to run their asses off going back and forth to haul the pallets, let 'em. We'll stand here and enjoy the refreshing sulfur-scented Surface air. It's not like there's a good job, so what difference does it make?" Mark nodded his head in Chapman's direction and he and Brown started unwrapping the pallets.

Mark watched as the shuttlecraft's big cargo doors slowly opened its monstrous jaws. When the doors were fully extended, he stepped to the edge of the doorway and looked down to the Surface dust below. The deck of the massive vehicle was at least twenty-five feet off the ground at its lowest point.

Mark's partner was starting to position his side of the first crate while grumbling something about doing all the work. Mark quickly grabbed the other side of the load and helped guide it down the rollers. "Sorry about that. I didn't know we were ready to go," Mark said.

The trainee grumbled an unintelligible reply. He obviously had no interest in talking, so Mark entertained himself by eavesdropping on the other team's conversation.

"The job I want is manning the blaster. We're back here in the stink, sweating our balls off, and Lucas gets to sit there in the turret hoping to incinerate some Surface Dwellers."

"I would hate to have to fire that thing though. Killing hundreds of people with the press of a button is a lot of responsibility, Chapman."

"If you get the order, you gotta do it," Chapman countered.

"It's not like the Dwellers are going to bite the hand that feeds them anyway, they aren't going to attack us; and if they fight among themselves over the supplies, I don't know why we care," Brown replied.

"I think the blaster is mostly a reminder of who's in charge," Chapman said.

"Did they show your class the pictures of the aftermath from when the WA used it?"

"Yeah. I heard about it growing up, but seeing all those people just . . . melted. It was gross."

After offloading three pallets of supplies, the work halted and the conversation took precedence. Mark stood with his hands on his hips just inside the massive cargo door. He looked out over the hundred or so Dwellers who were following at a safe distance behind the shuttlecraft. They knew that the blaster was enabled when the craft was on land, so the Dwellers stayed back, but their hunger compelled them to remain close enough to the shuttle to retrieve its contents.

"There are a lot of them out there today," Mark said. "Do we have enough cargo?"

"We drop the same weight in each region every time," Chapman answered. "They know they get three full pallets. I don't know why they're still begging. We don't offload again until the next drop zone."

"Every one of those men probably has two or three people to feed," Mark said.

"Whose fault is that?" Chapman laughed.

Mark ignored the judgmental comment. "We had a lot of mouths at school too, but we had a garden. I hope this isn't their only food source."

"Of course it is," Brown said. "This whole region has chemicals in the dirt. Nothing will grow here."

"Then we need to increase the supply to fill the demand," Mark's partner said forcefully.

Chapman laughed, "That's not up to us, dude. You know we have to carry out our orders exactly as they are given or we'll get strung up."

"So, all those people get nothing?" The Grumbler asked.

"Guess they should have gotten here quicker," Chapman replied. "Is this your first food drop? That's how it goes."

"If those were your people, you wouldn't be so righteous."

"Calm down, man. There's nothing we can do," Chapman said.

Mark wasn't a natural peacekeeper, but he was wearing Wentworth's tags and Wentworth would try to smooth things out, so he felt obligated to try. "Is this your region?" Mark looked more closely at the Grumbler and tried to remember if he had seen him before on the battleairship.

"I don't have to be in my region to see those people as people. They're freakin' people. And they're hungry." The Grumbler moved toward the next pallet and tried to move it to the rollers himself.

"Let go of that! You break orders and we're all going to get in trouble," Chapman yelled.

An announcement over the PA interrupted the argument. "Trainees, this is Captain Edwards. Our sensors detect a thermal spike in the Surface temperature. Return to your seats immediately to prepare for reconfiguration of the aircraft and takeoff."

"Shit!" Mark exclaimed under his breath as he, Chapman, and Brown darted toward the shuttlecraft cabin. The Grumbler stayed behind and continued to struggle with the crate.

"Forget it, man. We're leaving. Did you hear that? Cap says a flare-up is coming. You wanna get burned alive?" Chapman ran to where The Grumbler stood and tried to pull him toward the main cabin.

"Let go of me! There's time to get at least one more pallet out if you help me."

"I'm not getting thrown in the Brig because you want to play hero for a bunch of animals."

The Grumbler's temper boiled over. He launched his fist into Chapman's jaw and followed it with his elbow. Chapman staggered backwards a few steps; he blew blood bubbles out of his nose and tested his jaw. Chapman's lips moved. He bared his teeth and delivered a warning so feral that no one could hear it. He tackled the Grumbler, slamming him into the steel floor and when his head bounced, Chapman rebounded it and slammed it into the floor again.

"Hey, hey!" Mark yelled. "Knock it off!" He tried to pull Chapman off his prey.

Brown saw that The Grumbler was contained, so he joined in the fight, kicking him in the gut with the reinforced toe of his work boot. "That's for always being so high and mighty, school boy."

Mark could see that social class was determining loyalties. There was tension among the trainees who came from the WA Sponsored schools and the guys from unnamed regions. Grumbler must have come from a school like Mark's. He felt obligated to keep the guy from getting beaten, but also to prove that the educated cadets weren't soft.

"Why don't you try fighting someone who's standing up?" Mark taunted Brown.

The trainee, as tall as Mark, but skinnier, took a swing that Mark easily blocked. Mark knocked the wind out of his opponent with an uppercut to the solar plexus and swept the kid's legs. The scrawny coward slammed to the deck like a puppet with his stings cut. Mark was disappointed when he didn't get up for more.

A piercing, repetitive buzz bounced off of every hard surface in the cargo area to indicate that the bay doors were starting to close. Red flashing lights swirled through the scene adding to the sense of urgency.

"We're taking off, Chapman. Enough is enough. Cap gave orders for us to get back in our seats," Mark yelled with authority in his voice.

Chapman pressed his full body weight onto The Grumbler once more for emphasis and then got to his feet. As soon as the target opened up, Grumbler landed a solid kick in Chapman's midsection. The powerful impact was loud enough to be heard over the mechanics of the lower cargo door as it slowly moved toward the closed position for takeoff.

"You have so much sympathy for the Dwellers, maybe you should join them!" In one adrenaline-fueled motion, Chapman straightened up, grabbed the foot that had just kicked him, and began to drag his victim to the open door. The Grumbler tried to kick with his free leg and tried to anchor himself with his hands, but there was nothing to grab hold of as he slid across the smooth steel deck.

Mark knew that the fight had already gone too far. If they survived the flare-up, the others would go to the Brig and he would be expelled. Mark could live with that, but he couldn't live with letting a clown like Chapman win. Mark grabbed him by the collar of his uniform. "Get off him! What the hell are you doing? Have you lost your freakin' mind, Chapman?"

Mark registered the sound of the "CRACK" before he felt the blow of something hard across his back. He fell to his knees and caught himself with outstretched arms. Mark raised his eyes and all he could see of The Grumbler was a pair of hands gripping the cargo door from the outside of the craft. Mark reacted quickly and was able to get a firm grip of The Grumbler's wrist. Mark pulled his feet underneath him and straightened his legs for leverage to pull his partner back on board. His fellow trainee was able to rest his other forearm on the deck of the shuttle and Mark let go so he could use both arms to climb back aboard.

The dangling trainee looked up to see who had rescued him, then yelled a warning, "Your six!"

It was too late. Mark had been shoved from behind and was sent on a trajectory that shot him off of the shuttlecraft ahead of the other falling body.

Chapman watched the cargo door settle into the closed position. As the steel doors locked into place, the realization of what he had done suddenly made him sick. He burst into the cabin of the shuttlecraft where the rest of the crew was belted in for the flight back to the battleairship. He could see that the cockpit door was open and he shouted to be heard above the pulse engines, "Captain, abort the takeoff, we have a man overboard! Man overboard!"

Captain Edwards removed his headset and looked back toward the main cabin to find the source of the yelling.

"Man overboard!" Chapman screamed again.

The Second-In-Command calmly relayed the latest information from the thermal detector, "Captain, we have a reading of 990 degrees Celsius and rising—anticipating a core flare that could reach 1,000 feet within one mile of here in approximately two minutes."

"We have soldiers on the Surface, Sir!" screamed Chapman.

The Second-In-Command's voice was steady compared to Chapman's hysterical pleading. "Need a go/no-go decision right now, Captain."

"Prepare for takeoff," the Captain barked.

"Configuring for takeoff," the SIC echoed. "Let's get the hell out of here."

Chapman sat down and reluctantly fastened his seatbelt. He used his sleeve to wipe blood from his mouth and nose. "I thought we never left a man behind," he said to no one in particular.

"We can't save them. It was a long fall from the cargo door. They're probably already dead." Brown whispered from the next seat. "And they deserve what they got."

CHAPTER THREE

The Surface Dwellers were a lot dirtier up close.

Mark took a deep breath and systematically bent and rotated the joints in his extremities. He had landed on his left side. His shoulder and hip hurt terribly, but his spine seemed intact. As he exhaled a giant breath of air, he raised himself to a sitting position. The contents of his head felt liquefied and he tried to command stability by pressing his hands to each side of his soft-boiled egg.

The sound of the pulse engines of the shuttlecraft, his ride home, faded into the distance. Mark looked up and saw the contrail streaming from behind the shuttle. To his surprise, the straight line wasn't bending into a U. They weren't coming back.

"Wentworth, we have to run!" The Grumbler screamed. He was already on his feet and had already chosen a random direction.

For a moment, Mark had forgotten about the flare-up that was coming from the core.

"Oh, shit!" Mark scrambled to his feet. As he uttered the rude word, his conversation with the General popped into his mind, but Mark didn't have time to try to figure out what caused the association . . . he had to run.

Mark saw that The Grumbler had a fifty-yard head start. The hundred or so Dwellers who had come for supplies, were now getting a show. They stood still and watched the scene unfold with amazement. World Army trainees didn't fall from the sky every day and they didn't know what to make of it. Some of them searched the heavens for the inevitable return of the shuttlecraft. Mark couldn't allow them to stand around here and be killed by the flare-up.

"Listen to me! Listen—there is going to be a flare-up somewhere around here—someplace close. Run as far as you can and go as fast as you can!" Mark shouted.

The Dwellers didn't move. Mark noticed that they had formed lines. The supply bags had been opened and men were distributing equal portions to those who were waiting. No one seemed to comprehend the urgency of what Mark was yelling about.

"Get away from here! The shuttlecraft took off because a flare is coming! You have to run!"

No one followed Mark's directions, so he decided to lead by example. He started sprinting in the same direction that The Grumbler had gone. The other trainee was well ahead of Mark, but he was easy to pick out. The Surface Dwellers wore threadbare, dusty clothes made from natural fabrics. They were smaller in stature compared to the WA trainees, and the Surface men wore long hair and beards. Mark kept his eyes on the charcoal military uniform and the familiar bald head as he increased his speed. He wished that he hadn't had so much to drink last night—his boots felt weighted and his back hurt terribly where he had been struck a few minutes ago. It was a trifecta of adverse effects on his ability to sprint.

The Surface started to vibrate. Mark had never been near a flare before, but he knew the warning signs. He ran faster.

"Hey . . . Trainee!" He screamed. Mark didn't even know the name of the person he felt most attached to in this moment of horror.

Mark felt the Surface tremors grow stronger under his feet and now the Dwellers started running toward the cluster of campsites. There was no way to detect the exact site of the flare, but if the tremors could be felt, it would be close. The Dwellers felt safe at home and their instinct was to get there.

Without any further warning, the ground between Mark and the Grumbler opened up and belched a fifty-foot wide geyser of fire that was at least five hundred feet tall.

Mark gasped and felt his throat burn. The sulfur smell that permeated the Surface intensified and the flash of light blinded him just before he blacked out.

CHAPTER FOUR

"Battleship Two Zero, we are a half mile out, request clearance to land."

"Roger that shuttle, clear to land at Bay Door Six."

"Bay Door Six, roger that. We are on final approach."

"Welcome home, Captain Edwards."

The Captain of the shuttlecraft was sweating profusely. Not because he was nervous about executing a landing he had logged a thousand times, but because he was returning to the battleairship with two fewer crewmembers than he had on board when he departed.   His interrogation of the two trainee witnesses hadn't yielded a satisfying explanation as to how it happened and now his ass was hanging out all over the place. Both trainees claimed that they hadn't seen anything. Chapman said that he and Brown were moving the pallets toward the ramp when the load became unstable and fell on top of him, causing him to fall and smash his face into the deck. He said that Brown came to his aid and, sometime while they were distracted, the other two trainees disappeared from the shuttle.

The Captain glanced at his Second-In-Command. He looked worse than Edwards felt. The Captain flipped the switch that allowed him to be heard only by those aboard the shuttle.

"Gentlemen my principal duty as a Captain is protecting my crew. I failed in doing that today. When I debrief the General, I will bring him up to speed on the extenuating circumstances we faced on this mission.

At this time the core is too unstable to deploy a search and rescue for the MIAs. Their training has prepared them for challenges such as the one they currently face. As soon as it is safe, a team will be sent for them. Until such time, rest assured that the command decision to return the shuttle and the remainder of the crew to the safety of the battleairship was the right decision. If you are questioned about the incident, I urge you to be forthcoming in providing every detail that you can remember. None of you want to face General Court Martial, which, of course, would be the charge for felony treason against the WA or its GIs. That is all."

Captain Edwards unkeyed his mic and uttered curses under his breath. His SIC continued to perform his duties without making eye contact with his superior.

"I ordered the crew to get back in their seats," Captain Edwards said, almost as if he could produce a do-over.

In the back of the shuttle, Chapman and Brown looked like they were going to throw up. Everyone knew that being convicted of treason meant death.

Once the craft landed on the battleairship, the crew silently disembarked. Captain Edwards, the last to get off the vessel, reported to the bridge.

Edwards stood at attention and spoke in a loud, clear voice to a spot on the wall behind the General's head. The General allowed him to finish without interruption, but the moment Edwards concluded his report, Walthers slammed his fist against his desk, causing a riptide in the glass of water sitting near the epicenter of the quake. The sound was like a shot from an executioner's gun.

"Protocol states that you would call in an AWOL as soon as it was discovered!"

"The men were not AWOL, Sir. To be clear, they were lost in action. Our radio signal was interrupted by the flare, General. All of the avionics were going haywire."

"So you made a command decision to leave two of our men on the Surface?" The General mocked Edwards' clipped monotone delivery.

"Sir, I had four other souls on board and a thirty-million dollar shuttlecraft to protect. Trainees Chapman and Brown had already attempted to locate the fallen trainees with no success."

"You said that already. How do you know these trainees didn't defect? Is it possible that they are alive?"

"I don't know, Sir. We were right on top of the site where the flare originated. The coordinates are in the shuttle nav for the search and rescue team, Sir."

"There will be a search and a full investigation, but I will entrust it to someone far more capable than you, Captain." The General spit the last word.

"Sir, I think you'll find--"

"You are grounded until further notice. Report to Major Haggart for your interim assignment. Dismissed."

Captain Edwards saluted the General, spun on the ball of his foot, and marched from the office.

The General took his private tablet from his desk and called up the hologram of his Information Officer. "Make an announcement immediately that two trainees went AWOL . . . no . . . say MIA on the supply drop. As a result, the battleairship will be under curfew. No one is to leave their quarters except for meals and work details. The on board monitors will be disabled and speaking will be forbidden unless a superior addresses a subordinate. "

The General didn't wait for a reply before ending the communication.

He slammed his fist into the desktop for one more thunderous burst before gathering himself and sending a private message from his tablet.

CHAPTER FIVE

Mark heard a woman humming softly and his heart started pounding at an accelerated pace. She was here! He tried to open his eyes, but his stubborn eyelids wouldn't respond. He wanted to say her name, but his tongue seemed fused to the roof of his mouth. Mark lifted his right hand and explored the space beside him.

"I'm right here," the female voice reassured him.

Mark felt a soft, small hand clasp his and bring it to rest on her lap.

Mark tried to inhale deeply through his nose to see if he could detect the orange blossom fragrance from the Transition Tier, but when the air touched the inside of his nostrils, the pain told him that he was not between lifetimes. It didn't matter to Mark where he was because he was with her. He couldn't see her now, but he could picture every detail of how she looked the first time they met, three lifetimes ago, on Tier Three. He replayed the scene in his mind . . .

It had truly been love at first sight. In fact, Mark loved her before he ever saw her. The day he met her, an anxiousness and excitement woke him very early in the morning.

Mark and his two brothers were on summer break from school and he knew they wouldn't appreciate being awakened. Their parents were on a mission in the poorest hemisphere in their region, so the boys were on their own. Mark snuck outside and ran a few miles to work his body and clear his head.

He returned to the family's sprawling house and got busy in the well-appointed kitchen. Mark used the skills his mother had taught him to cook grits with butter and cheese, and then he fried and diced up some bacon. He used the left over grease for cooking the shrimp, adding parsley, scallions, and garlic for flavor. The boys hadn't had a breakfast so extravagant since they had been left on their own. Mark had wanted everything about that day to be celebrated. He knew that day was the marker between "before" and "after." A giant magnet was pulling him to his destiny.

Mark remembered how he had rushed his brothers through their morning routines so they could get to the shore. When the boys arrived, the scene was the same as it had been every other day that summer. Familiar faces occupied the beach territories that they had claimed the first day of break. Kids of all ages laughed and screamed in the water and on the shore. The supposed sun burned everything in sight with its seemingly friendly glow.

Mark's brothers passed a ball back and forth on the sand, taking occasional swims to cool off, but Mark sat perched on the beach. His head swiveled constantly looking for…something. He wasn't sure what.

Then, for seemingly no reason, he got to his feet and walked a hundred yards until he stood next to her. She wasn't surprised to see him, although they had never met before. Her black hair fell to the middle of her back and glistened in the sunlight. She was a foot shorter than Mark with an athletic build. Her golden brown eyes sparkled when she smiled and her shoulders lifted up as if they were attached to the upturned corners of her mouth. Mark wanted to see that full body smile every day for the rest of his life.

They sat next to each other on the sand and talked until after sunset.

When Mark's brothers went home, he stayed behind. The young couple shared their hopes and dreams and Mark promised to do everything he could to make all of her dreams come true. They had found genuine, abiding love. They feared nothing.

Mark slept with his hand safely in hers and the beautiful memory fresh in his mind.

CHAPTER SIX

The Surface healer hadn't been difficult for Lon to locate. He simply followed the groups of Dwellers who were carrying their wounded to the sorry excuse for a hospital. Lon knew that the shuttle wouldn't return directly following a flare-up and his fellow GI needed care immediately. The WA medics would have been best, of course, but Lon thought the primitive Surface shaman might be better than nothing. When the search and rescue team did come back for them, Lon planned to guide the shuttle crew to the hospital.

When his Good Samaritan deed was complete, Lon walked back to where the shuttle departed from the Surface. Even if he had to wait several hours, he wanted to be close to the coordinates of his last known location--where the shuttle crew would begin its search.

The closer he got to the flare point, the more acrid the air became. Lon pulled the collar of his shirt around his mouth and nose to try to filter the odor. As the day progressed, Lon grew tired of pacing and sat down in the vast, open terrain. In every direction, all he could see was flat, reddish-brown dirt. The only point of interest was the flare site, which was charred, steaming, and billowing fumes that had to be toxic.

Lon watched the sun inch across the sky until it disappeared. After it dipped below the far horizon, he accepted that he would have to spend the night on the Surface. He was starved and dehydrated, so he walked back to the town to steal some food and water.

Just when Lon thought that he had made a clean getaway, he heard a voice calling to his back.

"Hey there, son. You need help?"

Lon didn't look behind him. He sped up his pace.

"I can give you some company . . . if you need someone to talk to."

The voice was weak and shaky. Lon couldn't tell if it belonged to a man or a woman, but he continued to put space between himself and his pursuer in case it was a ploy of some sort.

"I know how easy you World Army boys . . . have it up there. When I came back here . . . it was a shock to my system after all those years . . . on a battleairship." The wavering voice came in spurts that indicated breathlessness. Then it mustered strength and delivered a well-rehearsed command with the self-assurance that came along with authority. "About face, Trainee."

Lon stopped and spun around.

"My goodness you're a fast one," the man said as he hobbled up to where Lon waited. "Heard that a couple of you went overboard on the supply drop today. I've been looking for you."

Lon sized up the old man. A strong sneeze could have blown him over. Lon decided that he was not a threat. "I'm going back to where the accident happened, so I'll be in place when the shuttlecraft comes back."

The old man looked up at the sky. "No one's comin' back tonight, Junior. You might as well sit down and eat that grub you stole and build us a fire. It's gonna get cold out here quick."

"I don't want to call any attention to myself."

"Then cover that reflective dome of a head of yours," the old man laughed. "Building a fire won't call attention to yourself. Wanderers build fires out here every night. And who do you think is payin' attention to you anyway?"

"You are, for one," Lon said as he inattentively palmed the top of his head. "I'm sorry about the food I took. I'd buy it if I had any money," Lon explained.

"That don't matter none. You only took a little. I saw ya. It'll be missed, but it won't kill anyone." The old man took a long time to lower himself to the ground. He started to unpack his sack and patted the dirt beside him. "I have some stolen food myself. Enough for me to survive, but not so much that anyone will suffer for the loss of it. Sit down here and we two thieves will have dinner together."

"I think I will sit with you, Gramps." The idea of getting off his feet suddenly appealed to Lon very much. "So, you expect me to believe that you've been aboard a WA airship?" Lon asked. He stretched out in the dirt, lying on his back with his knees pointed toward the sky.

"Believe it or don't, I don't care. I spent eighteen years on number nine. I was the best cook they had. Ran the whole kitchen. Name's Napoli. My men called me Nappy." The old man held out his dry grain. "Not much I can do with this to make it taste better, but I was once a cook."

Lon was skeptical. "Yeah? Then what happened?"

"I retired. Now I'm seeing the world."

"That's not what WA retirees do. My Dad was a Master Sergeant. After his service, the Army gave him a house in their sponsored Surface community. He got married and had his allotment of children--me. With a retirement set-up like that, there's no way someone would choose to be a Wanderer instead." Lon sat up and drank the water he stole in one gulp.

"It was wonderful when I was young and knew everything like you do," the old man smiled.

"So, after eighteen years, you came back down here and . . . what? Opened a grain kitchen?"

"My wife waited eighteen years for me. We were too old to have children by the time I came back from duty, so we stayed in the town where we both grew up. It was a lovely town until the WA incinerated it."

Lon's stomach clenched. "I'm really sorry. Was your wife . . . ?"

"Killed. Yup. The Army I served killed the person I loved the most."

Lon didn't know what to say. "I'm really sorry," he repeated.

"It's been a long time ago, now. And I don't blame anyone. I don't blame you for servin' the Army. It's a good life. You're a legacy so your old man knew that."

"Yeah. He shaped me from a young age. He said service to the WA was the difference between a comfortable life and a life of struggle."

"I guess that's true for men who need to have material things to feel comfortable," Nappy said gnawing on his grain. "So, do your folks still live in the WA community? Is it close to here?"

"We lived in another hemisphere, but when Dad died, they evicted me and Mom. Said retiree benefits die with the retiree. We went back to where my mom grew up. I hated leaving her there when I signed on for training. It's a desolate place. Every time I sit down to a hot meal or go to sleep in my soft bed aboard the ship I feel guilty as sin, but she wouldn't let me turn down the commission."

"You have a good mother. She's fulfilled by her son's good fortune."

"I guess."

"Are you scared?" the old man asked.

"Of what?"

"All of it. Wanderers who would kill you for your belongings, the Army not comin' back for ya, never seein' your Mom again . . ."

"I guess," Lon said again quietly. Then he sat up straighter and popped some grain into his mouth. "No, not really. I'm not scared. I'll be fine."

"You should take my coat," the old man said. "It'll cover that uniform. Your head is glowing like a lantern in the moonlight, but I don't have a hat to cover that up. It will take a while for your hair to grow out, but when it does, you won't stand out so much."

"I'll be back on the ship long before that happens," Lon said. "And it gets cold at night, so you need that coat more than I do."

"Wonderful to be young and know everything," Nappy said again, slapping Lon on the back. "Speaking of the cold, build me a fire, son. There's some broken up pieces to burn in this bag here." The older man tossed the sack in front of them.

Lon had a lighter in his pocket, which made quick work of the project.

"Don't let anyone see that, Trainee. They'll kill you for it."

"I wouldn't take it out in front of a Dweller. And I don't have to use it, I know how to start a fire from flint—I paid attention in my survival classes. But I'm not worried about using up the butane since I won't be down here long."

The old man chuckled and wrapped up the rest of his uneaten grain. "There's a blanket in that sack too. Can you hand it to me?"

Lon opened the sack and used the soft glow of the fire to find the threadbare blanket.

"Do you think there's a way to contact the battleairship from the Surface, Nappy?"

"Someone must know how. The Army raided a Surface town a few months ago, or maybe it was a few years ago . . . A Dweller informed the Army that a town here was making weapons. Can't blame the Dweller— the Army was withholding supplies until they found out where the guns were coming from. Dweller probably saw his kids starving and couldn't take it anymore. Anyway, someone knows how to do it, but that someone isn't me, son." Nappy was quiet for a minute. "You'll probably be gone by the time I wake up, so thanks for the company," Nappy said sleepily.

"Where are you heading tomorrow?" Lon asked.

"It doesn't matter. I'll follow my feet and lay down when I get tired," the old man said closing his eyes.

Lon slept soundly and woke up at the first light of day. Nappy was still asleep and Lon didn't want to wake him. He left his lighter in the old man's sack and took his coat. He felt it was an even exchange and the former WA cook had offered it to him. The next person who pegged Lon for an Army GI might not be as friendly as Nappy. Lon looked down at the man for a long minute, put on the ankle-length coat, and walked into whatever events the day had waiting for him.

CHAPTER SEVEN

"Try to open your eyes. The plant jelly has reduced the swelling considerably, so I think you can," Mark heard the lilting voice instruct him.

"Let me see your eyes, Mark Mead Wentworth," Mark was shocked to hear his name combined with Wentworth's and the memory of taking his place came rushing back to him.

"Baby?" His throat felt dry and a sponge filled with moisture touched his lips.

"Shhh. Try opening your eyes. That will be progress."

Mark opened his eyes and saw that a bald woman with tan skin and light blue eyes was smiling at him. Mark could feel kindness radiating from her. He started to cry when he realized that this woman was a stranger to him.

"It's okay. It's all right," she said softly. "You've been through a lot in the last two days and you probably have as many emotions about it as you have questions. I will tell you what I know about how you arrived here if you promise not to talk anymore. Your vocal cords are swollen and scorched. Now that you are awake, I can place some roots under your tongue and I'm sure you will be able to speak normally in a few days. I am Ellie." The woman smiled again and Mark noticed that parentheses formed on either side of her mouth when she did. The skin around her eyes crinkled a bit as well. She was older than him by at least twenty years, maybe more, but she was beautiful.

"Your fellow trainee, Lon Walker, brought you to our town yesterday morning. You slept all day, through the night, and all day again today. This is your second night with us."

Mark thought that Lon Walker was a much better name for the kid who saved his life than "The Grumbler." Mark composed himself and nodded slightly, hoping to learn more.

"Lon said that you had helped him fight off an attack on the shuttlecraft and got thrown overboard as a result. He felt responsible for making sure that you didn't get burned alive in the flare-up." Ellie wrung out the sponge that she had touched to Mark's lips. The water trickled into a large glass that contained about two tablespoons of water. The drops barely raised the water level, but Ellie carefully collected the liquid.

"Your friend Lon wouldn't stay with us. He felt that the shuttlecraft would be back for you, but there have been no signs of any World Army crafts in the area." Ellie placed her hands in her lap. Mark realized that she was sitting on the bare ground and that a thin straw mat was the only thing between him and the dirt. "No one has heard anything about him or seen him since he brought you to the town."

"I am the closest thing we have to a healer. I am familiar with the properties of herbs and other natural remedies, but mostly I provide comfort. You weren't badly hurt, but you were very close to the flare. The intense heat and flash of light combined with the chemical reaction that occurs within the Surface soil shocked your system. You were exposed to some radiation, I'm sure, but you should feel like yourself again very soon."

"I imagine, once the core settles down, the Army will come back for you and I want them to see that we have taken good care of you." Ellie smiled and searched Mark's eyes.

"What other questions would I have if I were you, Mark Mead Wentworth? I'm not sure that is your name—is it?" Mark shook his head and Ellie giggled.

"Your fellow trainee called you Wentworth and your I.D. tags say Wentworth, but the WA currency card that I found in your pocket says *Mark Mead.*" Mark nodded slightly.

"I thought so! Your fellow trainee was so sure that your name was Wentworth. How many soldiers must you have on those massive airships if you don't even know each other?" Ellie wondered out loud. "I know every soul here. There are almost a thousand of us now. My husband, Jonas, and I have two children. John age 12, and Sarah is 10."

Hearing about Ellie's family reminded Mark of his love and the memory hurt more than the various pains in his body.

"We work together for the common good. Jonas and John carry water from the source to the town and Sarah cares for children so the parents can contribute . . . but you are probably too tired to absorb any more information now. You are very healthy, but you will need to eat soon to regain your strength. Rest and heal so you will be able to swallow nourishment tomorrow." Ellie motioned for Mark to lift his tongue and she placed some strong smelling powder in his mouth. "Just let that reconstitute naturally and swallow normally. I'll be back to check on you tomorrow."

Mark didn't want Ellie to leave, but she had other patients to comfort. For the first time, Mark looked around at his surroundings. There were several Dwellers lined up on either side of him. Some were covered with terrible burns, some had missing limbs, and others moaned restlessly. One lay far too still. Mark decided that sleep was his refuge. Well after the long night turned into day, Mark allowed himself to remain in semi-conscious oblivion.

* * * *

"You like to believe the best about everyone, Ellie. That is one of the many things that I love about you, but we cannot invite the unknown into our home. If we didn't have the children to consider, I might agree, but it would be irresponsible. We will find other ways to help Mark."

Mark heard a man with a deep, strong voice speak his name, but he didn't have the will to wake up, so he dozed, half listening to what was going on around him. The man spoke deliberately and with conviction, but not forcefully.

"He shouldn't be this weak. I think the emotional wound is deeper than his physical ailments. He should be entirely back to normal by now, as young and as fit as he is. His burns were very superficial, like a bad burn from a far-off supposed sun. He is already healed physically, yet he isn't willing to be well."

"You are assuming that he's an innocent soul in need of help, Ellie. There is a reason the Army ejected him and left him here. They invested time and money into him. He's their possession, but they tossed him aside. That isn't much of a character reference if you ask me."

Mark heard Ellie's soft giggle. "There are no mistakes. How many times have you told me that? He fell from the shuttle into our region. He was injured just enough to be brought directly to me—to us. And he keeps mumbling about the Journeys, searching for someone, and the Transition Tier. There are very few Knowers on this Tier, Jonas, and yet he found us. So, I'm supposed to ignore these truths? I can't just shake his hand and say good-bye."

"Of course not, but we must consider that the children--"

"Will learn more from our example than our lectures. He was guided to us, Jonas. You know as well as I do that he belongs here. With us. This world can harden a man's heart, but surely not a heart as loving as yours."

For a moment it was quiet and Mark wondered if the couple had left.

"Of course you're right."

Ellie giggled again. "I know that I have evolved past this point, but I still love being right. To hear my husband admit that I am right makes it so much sweeter."

"Now who's letting this world influence them?" Jonas teased.

CHAPTER EIGHT

Mark devoured the tasteless soaked grain that Ellie had brought for him as if it were a rare delicacy. He hadn't realized how hungry he was until he started eating.

"I wish I could offer you more water, but we won't receive another supply drop until next week and we have to ration what we have. The water we have here is not potable," Ellie explained.

Mark gulped the grain and carried on the conversation simultaneously, "There's a water source here?"

"Yes. Jonas and our son John are water carriers. They carry containers of water from the source into town. That is a prestigious job—the carriers are rewarded with housing. When John was born, Jonas had the foresight to put him on the carrier list. It's nice to have the peace of mind to know that John and Sarah will be able to remain in the house after we pass."

"Has there been any news of Lon?" Mark was excited to feel alive again—to eat, have a conversation, and to ask the questions that had been percolating in his mind. Ellie kept pace with the varying topics he brought up.

"No. Don't let that worry you though. There are wanderers who prey on people traveling alone, but, with his Army training, Lon should be able to handle himself."

"I just don't know why they wouldn't have come back for us."

"Perhaps the core is more unstable than we realize. We have no way of predicting a flare. By the time we feel it, the blast is inescapable."

Mark scooped the last bit of grain from the bowl that Ellie had given him when she arrived.

"Thank you for the food and for making me well," Mark said.

"Of course. Now that you are better, do you have a plan?" Ellie asked.

"I guess I'll set out to find Lon."

"Would you consider staying with us?"

"I don't want to impose—I've already eaten a day's worth of your food."

"Don't worry about that." Ellie stood up and held her hand out to Mark. He hadn't been on his legs since the day of the flare and he got dizzy when he first stood up. Apart from a moment of unsteadiness, Mark felt pretty good.

"Come with me, I want to show you around. The children are contributing, but Jonas is at home. I'll take you to the house and you can decide if you'd like to settle in with us." Ellie led the way. The tented area where the sick were was about two hundred yards outside of the shantytown.

Mark had seen the settlement from above, but walking the streets gave him a feel for what couldn't be grasped from his former perspective.

There was a sense of order in this place. Here, among the dust and the Surface grime, among mismatched building materials, and in spite of the seemingly miserable living conditions, every citizen moved with purpose.

With each lifetime, Mark matured earlier and earlier. He became aware of universal truths and his powers of observation were acute enough for him to feel what newer souls might not even notice. Mark braced himself for the anger, despair, and fear that he imagined would generate from the Dwellers. Instead, he was filled with love, joy, and energy.

Ellie walked beside Mark and greeted each person they passed by name, but Mark noticed that many looked the other way or did not respond.

"Is it going to cause trouble for you and your family if I stay with you? I'm probably not going to be super popular here."

"Our people are loving, but they're cautious. Once they see that Jonas and I trust you, they will accept you."

"Does Jonas trust me? I overheard you talking at the hospital. It seemed like you had to talk him into letting me stay with you," Mark said.

Ellie greeted another friend and then turned back toward Mark, "Jonas is vey wise. His heart is wide open, but he is also protective. He has seen things that have made him this way," she explained.

Mark felt that he shouldn't pry further. They had walked through the area of town where the dwellings were more like outdoor campsites and now a row of about fifty small houses, all attached to each other, formed a boundary marking the far edge of the town. The homes were all the same color of natural wood, aged by the supposed sun and caked with Surface grime. They were all in disrepair. Roofs were warped, front steps crumbled, and several front doors hung from their hinges.

In the path in front of the row housing, a group of small boys, all around age nine or younger, played a game with a ball. One of the boys, a blond with vibrant blue eyes looked up from his game and waved to Mark. When Mark didn't wave back, the boy laughed and pointed at him, then waved again. Mark smiled back and waved a weak little wave— something like the salute he hadn't mastered.

Ellie gave Mark a hint on how to find their door, "Coming from the center town road, the one we were just on, you count four doors to the right. Don't count steps because not all of the houses have them anymore. Four doors to the right is our castle." Ellie climbed three squat stairs and opened a solid door that was well balanced on adequate hinges. "King, your queen has returned!" She shouted loudly and needlessly. Her husband sat at a table less than twelve inches from her toes.

Jonas laughed and shook his head. "Welcome home, Your Highness. Welcome, Mark."

Jonas stood up to shake Mark's hand. He was several inches shorter than Mark and older than Ellie, but he was a force of a man. His presence was intimidating. Mark's first impression was that Jonas would make an excellent General in the World Army.

"Thank you, Sir. Thank you for your hospitality. I don't intend to impose on you for too long." Mark could see the entire one-room house from where he stood. Four people were already living in an area only a little bit larger than his quarters on the battleairship.

The table that Jonas had been sitting at had four mismatched chairs around it and a fat candle with three wicks in the center of it. There was a cabinet with a countertop where four glasses of various shapes and sizes sat beside a stack of four bowls with four spoons arranged in the top one. There was a pitcher less than half-full of water on the cupboard as well. A piece of cardboard placed over the top kept out the dust. Mark saw a stack of neatly folded blankets in the corner of the room. The house was elevated and had a wood floor. Mark noticed that there was no Surface dirt inside the house. He felt stupid—Ellie had taken off her shoes at the bottom of the front steps and he had worn his boots inside.

"Oh, I'm so sorry!" He ran back down the steps, removed his boots and returned to where Ellie and Jonas were chuckling together. "Do you have a broom? I tracked dirt inside."

"Thank you for being so considerate, but there is no harsh punishment for bringing dirt inside, "Ellie assured him.

"We can take care of that later. Please, sit down." Jonas took his seat at the table again.

Mark reacted as if the suggestion was an order. And, although the walk hadn't been a long one by military training standards, he was a still a little shaky from having been on his back for the last few days. He was happy to sit. Ellie sat in a chair beside him that was slightly taller than Mark's, elevating her to the highest position at the table.

"Ellie tells me that you were mumbling a bit while you slipped in and out of consciousness at the hospital. You spoke of the Journeys. You are aware that you have lived before?"

Mark was too stunned to speak. No one in any other lifetime had ever talked to him about the Journeys. He nodded his reply.

"Your soul collects experiences, knowledge, and memories with each Journey. It stands to reason that you would become more aware of the growth process as you proceed through the lifetime Tiers," Jonas said.

"You can talk to us, Mark. Jonas and I are Knowers. We proceeded through the Tiers to Enlightenment. There is nothing you can tell us that we don't already know, but if you can help us understand where you are in your Journeys, it will help us not to divulge things to you that you may not be ready for yet."

"I was on the battleairship and then I fell here . . ." Mark didn't know where to start.

"There are no accidents, Mark. Do you believe that?" Jonas asked patiently.

"Yes."

"You are here because you were guided here."

"Yes," Mark agreed. "Um, okay then." Mark exhaled a big breath of air through puffed cheeks. "Two lifetimes before this one, I met my soul mate on Tier Three. I knew that we were meant to travel together through the remaining Tiers until we reached Enlightenment, but at the end of our Journey on Tier Three, we were separated."

Jonas nodded to encourage Mark to continue.

"In my next lifetime, I remembered her around the time I was 15. I searched for her relentlessly. I consciously worked to stay on the frequency of love that we had shared. I tried to attract her to me. I tried to manifest my wish to be with her into reality. Nothing worked. Time being relative, it was a very long, very hard existence. I didn't start paying attention to anything on the Tier until I had grown very old. The lessons of the Journey didn't begin until I was very close to my expiration date.

I didn't make the same mistake on Tier Five. I focused on my lesson, but never gave up looking for her. I thought that we were on the same Path because we were two halves of one soul, but I didn't find her there either.

I appealed after the Fourth and Fifth Tier, but The Spirit told me to increase my faith. It seems it isn't His will for us to be together, but, loving me as He does, I cannot understand Him keeping me in this pain. I was sure that it had been decided that we would stay together."

Ellie and Jonas exchanged glances and Jonas covered Ellie's small hand with his large one.

"I think that we can help you, Mark. I can see that your current situation, being left behind by the Army, is just a footnote of a much bigger story. You will need to be patient. And you will have decisions to make. If the Army comes back for you, will you return to them? If you don't go, you will have to run or you may face being charged with desertion. Also, if I help you, you need to understand that I will ask something of you in return. Our society relies on a barter system. You will be indebted to me," Jonas said.

"I wasn't going to enlist in the Army after training. If they come back for me, after the core settles down, I'll deal with that, but it seems like the WA is not in a hurry to get me back." Mark smiled. "As far as being indebted to you, ah . . . I'll do what I'm capable of to repay your kindness. I've never met a Knower before—I didn't realize there were enlightened people," Mark moved his hands in circular motions in front of him, "down here."

Jonas and Ellie laughed.

"There is much that we can teach you, but we also have practical matters to address. We will need to trade for more grain and you will want a soft roll or blanket for bedding. Your military uniform would probably fetch a few week's worth of nourishment for the family."

"Sure. I'd be happy to sell it," Mark offered eagerly.

"What trinkets do you have in your pockets?" Jonas asked.

Mark emptied his pockets onto the table. He realized as he did that Ellie had already been through his belongings, but everything he had on the shuttlecraft was still there. His lip balm, his WA currency card, and Wentworth's tags. Mark picked up the tags and rubbed them between his fingers. He felt overwhelming sadness that he would probably never see his friend again. Wentworth was the closest "family" he'd had for the last thirteen years. Mark's sadness quickly turned to laughter as he realized that Wentworth would have had to assume his identity or their unlawful switch would be exposed. Poor Wentworth, the one most concerned about his World Army training record had just inherited the spottiest record in their class. Mark wondered if his buddy would acquire a taste for drink.

"So, how do I go about trading this stuff?"

"You've had enough activity for this morning. Give me your uniform, wrap up in the children's blankets, and take a nap in the bedroom." Ellie gestured toward the corner of the one room house. "Jonas knows who to go to—he'll get the best price for the uniform."

"Take this stuff too." Mark slid the contents of his pockets towards Jonas.

"I'll take the lip balm. That kind of luxury will buy us some water. Keep the IDs. You might need them."

"Thank you . . . for all of this. I'm actually pretty excited to be here," Mark said.

"The children love the idea of you staying with us too. Everyone in town knows about the WA soldiers that fell from the sky. It scares the adults to have you in our town, but there is an awful lot of curiosity about you among the kids." Ellie said.

Mark remembered the little boy with the blond hair. Somehow, knowing the child was close by bolstered Mark's faith.

CHAPTER NINE

The first night in Jonas and Ellie's home left Mark surprisingly well rested and very inspired. After a small breakfast, each of the family members went off to contribute, leaving Mark alone on the congested path in front of the house. He was determined to fit into the community, but his conspicuous physical appearance didn't help matters. Mark wore high-water pants that Ellie had gotten off a corpse the day before, with a vest that Jonas usually wore over his own shirt. He looked like the victim of a science experiment that increased him to three times his normal size overnight.

Mark was several inches taller than the tallest Surface Dweller—he had been able to nourish his growth spurts-- and he was far healthier-looking and stronger than any of the Surface Dwellers. His body was well developed thanks to daily conditioning. He hadn't been on the dusty Surface for long enough to accumulate the amount of soot they wore, so his appearance was far neater. Mark took a moment to be consciously grateful for his blessings.

The main road led Mark past families working in various ways. Signs posted in front of the camps indicated that some families specialized in useful trades like clothing repair, weaving, and melting down metals.

As Mark walked past, the people peeked at him with curiosity and fear. He tried to make eye contact or smile, but no one gave him the chance.

Mark had almost given up on finding a way to contribute when he noticed a man struggling to balance a small half-barrel of water above his head. Mark could see the water sloshing over the lip of the container and, knowing how precious water was, he couldn't stand the sight. He rushed over to help.

"I have it, I have it," Mark assured the man. "What were you trying to do with it?"

The man, at least forty years older than Mark, cleared his throat. "I was trying to sit it on that pedestal I built up there." He pointed about twelve inches above his head.

Mark lifted the barrel into place. "Like that?"

"Yup, just like that." The man wiped his dusty hand on his dusty pant leg and held it out to Mark. "I'm Dean. Thanks for the help."

"I'm Mark. I'm staying with Jonas and Ellie's family," he added to give himself some credibility.

"I know who you are. You're about the only man in the town tall enough to reach the top of that pedestal. I built her lying down and I lay down next to her to see how high my arms could reach, but I didn't take into account that I'm not as strong as I used to be. Lifting the heavy barrel over my head was . . . well, you showed up right on time." Dean smiled.

"You store your water up there then?"

"That was the plan. Keeps the snakes out. And if you can slide the cover on for me . . ." Dean handed Mark a circular shaped piece of particle board, " . . . that will keep the dust out."

Mark slid the lid into place and looked around Dean's camp. There were five more pedestals laying side by side in a tight row.

"You plan on needing more storage?" Mark asked.

"Well, they all think I'm crazy," the man said loud enough for his neighbors to hear, but I'm building a water filtering system so I can change the dirty water to good. They'll all be in line to get some once I get it workin'!" he shouted.

"We had one of those at the school I went to."

"You've actually seen a working model?"

"Yeah, it didn't work as often as it did, but we were happy to have it."

"So, such a thing exists?"

"Sure. It removed the impurities through several different filters. The process worked pretty well. Is that the type you're building?"

"I knew it!" Dean shouted with joy. "I knew it, I knew it, I knew it, I knew it!" he sang as he danced around.

"Let me make sure I understand. You aren't copying a design you've actually seen? You came up with the concept yourself?"

"Yup. I knew it could be done and you can show me how!" Dean pointed at Mark's chest.

"Well, I didn't build the filtration system at the school, but I'm pretty handy. If I had the right parts, I bet I could help you build one."

Dean grabbed Mark by the arm and dragged him to the rear of his campsite where a multitude of parts and pieces were carefully laid out on a tarp.

"I got everything we need to get started and maybe even to finish her," he said. "I just needed the final piece of the puzzle and it's you, boy, so let's get goin'. You showed up right on time," Dean said again for emphasis.

"All right. You've got yourself a helper. Let's see your materials."

Mark heard footsteps approaching and looked over his shoulder. The young blond boy who had waved to him yesterday walked through the campsite to where Dean and Mark were standing.

"Hi there youngun'," Dean greeted the boy.

"Hi-ho," the boy replied as if the exchange was familiar. He looked up at Mark. "Hey."

Mark smiled broadly and bent down to shake hands with him. The touch validated the easy connection between them.

The boy's face lit up. "See you later!" He shouted in the excited way that young boys say everything. His dashing feet left poufs of dust clouds in his wake.

The two would-be inventors went back to sifting through the parts and pieces that Dean had collected. Mark tried to categorize the scraps and set aside the bits that were entirely useless while Dean preached.

"You see why we need to filter the water—it's the best option we have for cleanin' it. Boilin' it ain't practical—it takes too much time to hold the water at a boil, let it cool down, aerate it for taste, and all that busy work. By the time you can take a sip, you're already dehydrated. And you'd need to do it all day long, which would run you out of stuff to burn by day two." Dean's grammar wasn't the best, but he spoke with the same conviction as the WA Majors who lectured the trainees.

"People here get desperate and try to steal the water brought to town by the Carriers. They usually get diarrhea, most times become pretty sick, and frequently die."

"I've been watching this for decades and I knew if I found the right way to separate the waste from the water, I could convert the bad water to potable water. I know you Army boys use chemicals to clean your water and you want to keep us dependent on your engineered fluid, but it's better sense to go natural and be self-sufficient."

"Don't go lumping me in with the bad guys in your conspiracy theory," Mark laughed. "You can't blame me for accepting a clean berth on a state-of-the-art cruise ship for a couple years of easy living. As far as your water filtration system goes, you have the right idea, I'm just not sure you have the right parts to make it work."

"If I don't have what I need, I probably have what I need to get it." Dean turned around and took a few steps before he realized that Mark wasn't following. "What are you waitin' for? Let get goin'!"

Dean walked Mark to a neighboring camp to barter with a family who collected fragments like he did. The family knew that the crazy old man had finally met his match when Mark explained the types of parts he thought he might need to complete the water filter. Mark hoped to obtain clean natural filters with small enough pores to block protozoa and bacteria, but he settled for two aluminum buckets. The containers would be handy for collecting the water at various stages of filtration and the buckets would be easier to sterilize than Dean's old barrel.

The water filtration system at the WA school had a pump to expedite the process. Mark made it a priority to find two pieces of rubber that could be used as flappers. Instead, he and Dean found pipe and hoses. They were necessary components for the pump, but Mark was frustrated that none of their acquired puzzle pieces fit together. Dean told Mark not to worry and walked with him to Jonas' house. Dean hadn't stopped smiling, laughing, or bragging all day. If Mark's life mission had been to fill Dean's spirit, he would have been back at the Transition Tier by now.

Ellie was the only one home when Mark got back, which made him feel as if he hadn't contributed enough to call it a day.

"What can I do to help?" he asked as he watched Ellie prepare the family dinner.

"Have a seat and talk to me," she answered. "One of my favorite people died today and I'm sad. I need to change my frequency. I know that I need to love her enough to be happy for her transition. I know that I am with her right now in Enlightenment. I know that this time and place is nothing more than an illusion, but I feel emotional rather than logical right now," she explained.

"Okay. Should I change the subject completely then?"

"Whatever you want to talk about is fine." Ellie smiled as she portioned out the servings. There was a fifth mismatched place setting now, one that Jonas had negotiated for.

"Did you choose this Tier and this situation?" Mark asked.

"Yes. The people here pray with such courage and faith. Answering their call was important to us."

"So, you and Jonas came here together, you didn't meet here?"

"That is correct. We came together." Ellie spoke slowly and softly.

"As newborns or can you arrive at any stage of development?"

"You can talk to us more freely than we can give you information. It is important that I do not provide insight into lessons you haven't learned yet because that will adversely affect your Journey."

"Oh." Mark thought for a moment. "But it is possible to travel together through Tiers?"

"Only after you reach Knowing in Enlightenment," Ellie said gently. "Or unless it is part of the Plan." She finished mixing the grain with the water, covered it, and left it on the counter to soak. Ellie pulled a chair out from the table and sat across from Mark.

"What if she forgets me? Or if she connects with another soul?"

"The soul connection happens once. You may share love with many, but your soul will truly connect with only one other soul," Ellie assured him.

"I can't wait until Enlightenment," Mark said matter-of-factly.

"We will talk about this more when Jonas can be with us. He is better at explaining things than I am." Ellie changed the subject. "Tell me, how are you getting along with Dean? He is a character, isn't he?"

"Yeah. He's a good guy. He had an idea about building a filter to clean Surface water and it can be done. Without having seen a working filtration system, he knew it was possible. He's smarter than people think he is."

"When his wife died, he had enough love to rejoice her passing. The people of the town thought his reaction was unnatural and they thought he had lost his mind. Ever since then, he has been labeled," Ellie explained.

"What about his son? How did he react when his mother died?" Mark asked.

"Dean doesn't have a son."

"But the boy that I met at Dean's, I assumed that--,"

Ellie leaned over to Mark's side of the table and took his hand into her own, "Before you Know, you will give birth to many flawed assumptions." She smiled.

CHAPTER TEN
REMEMBERING TIER THREE

The sound of her voice made Mark's spirit soar. When she said his name, he felt happier than he had ever thought was possible. He worked constantly to provide her with the same joy, but he doubted that he would ever accomplish that goal.

"Good morning sleepyhead," she sang softly as she covered his face with sweet kisses. When she leaned close to him, Mark could smell the orange blossom rinse she used in her hair. "I finished."

Mark's eyes sprang open and he leaped from the bed in a single motion. "You finished it?"

She nodded and clasped her hands together with her fingers intertwined they way she always did when she was excited.

"Is it everything you hoped it would be?" Mark asked

"It's my masterpiece," she whispered. "Come see."

Mark followed her from the bedroom and down the hall to the studio. The exterior wall facing the water was made entirely of glass sliding doors, which she kept open. The salty breeze kept the room cool and it smelled of sea air. This was her natural habitat.

The finished masterpiece stood in the center. It was a statue that she had carved from a piece of solid ivory. It was so tall that she had to climb a ladder and balance there for countless hours while she expertly coaxed the piece to life.

It was Mark, standing strong and tall, holding her in his arms. The ivory was pure white, lending an angelic hue, but it was the facial expressions of the subjects that were breathtaking. The eyes contained emotion and their feelings were unmistakable. She wore a lace shawl, the details of which had taken nearly a year to complete. Mark saw love and patience in every square inch of the sculpture. The longer he looked at it, the more he appreciated the complexity of the details. He had been interested in the work from the day she selected the ivory and he had enjoyed watching her progress. But the finished product was better than the sum of its parts. It was unlike anything he had ever seen before. Her statues were so unique that people gladly waited years for work they commissioned her to do, and paid her obscene amounts of money to own it.

"You are my muse, Mark. I could never have imagined this if I hadn't felt it first," she cooed as she snuggled under his arm.

"We can't sell this." He pulled her closer to him and she giggled.

"We have to sell it. This will pay the baby's way through Higher Education," she reminded him, placing a hand on her bulging stomach. "Ah! He wants us to sell it, Mark. He just kicked!" She laughed and placed Mark's hand where the action was.

"All right, all right. We'll sell your masterpiece to your client, but I want millions of pictures and hours video of it before we let it go."

"Of course," she promised.

"I have to go to work, Love. Just as the world is made more beautiful by your art, the world cannot do without my grease-monkey skills," Mark joked.

"Your talent helps people every day. It directly affects their lives. You make the difference between whether they can drive to work or have to walk. What I do only makes the world more beautiful."

"Thanks for trying to make me feel important, but I don't want to live in a world without beauty." Mark kissed her forehead, each cheek, and lingered at her lips. He bent down and spoke to his son, "You have the most amazing mother, son, but don't come out to meet her until Daddy has a day off."

CHAPTER ELEVEN

When Wentworth heard the announcement from the Information Officer, he had a gut feeling that Mark was one of the two who went missing during the supply drop. When an hour, then another hour, then another passed, and Mark didn't come bursting into his quarters spewing the wild story of what happened, Wentworth's fear was confirmed.

Mark's work schedule was posted in his quarters and Wentworth reported to the machine shop at the designated times to avoid suspicion, but his hope for ever seeing his friend again declined with each passing day.

Four days after Mark had not returned from the trip to the Surface, Wentworth was desperate for information. Under the current curfew restrictions, it was impossible to hear any news related to the disastrous Surface mission.

At the last meal of the day, he took a huge risk and slipped a note to the trainee who sat beside him in the Mess. The trainee had been on the trip to the Surface. The note simply said:

What happened to Mark Mead?

The trainee read the note and looked directly at the guy to his right for the first time since the incident. His eyes filled with panic when he realized it wasn't Mark beside him. He focused on his plate again and whispered without moving his lips, "Meet me in the locker room in fifteen minutes. I have cleaning detail. There are about thirty of us. You won't be noticed."

Wentworth hadn't had an appetite lately, so he carried his full dinner tray to the trash, scraped his plate and went to the locker room where he locked himself in a stall until he heard the cleaning crew arrive. The detail had begun their work in silence, but once the soldier in charge of them had left, it had gotten loud. Wentworth hadn't heard voices for a couple days and it was great to hear guys having normal conversations. Blending into the action, he made his way from the stall and washed his hands at the sink while using the mirror in front of him to scan the faces hard at work behind him.

"Hey." The kid from the Mess approached Wentworth and waved him over to a corner where they could speak privately. "So, who the hell are you, man?"

"Wentworth. Mark was my buddy. We went to the same school together on the Surface. We had each other's backs."

"Yeah. Mark was that kind of guy," the kid agreed. "My name is Lucas. He always gave me his dessert. I can't believe I didn't realize that he was the one on the Surface drop mission. I sit next to the guy three times a day and I didn't even notice."

"He didn't want to be noticed; he was filling in for me. I didn't want to go, so he went instead," Wentworth's voice cracked and he had to clear his throat to regain his composure. "So, what happened?"

Lucas looked around to make sure that none of the other trainees were within earshot before he began. "I wasn't in the cargo area. I'm trained on the blaster, but Wen—Mark and three other guys got sent back there to off load. About ten minutes into the drop, the Captain came on the PA and said they detected a flare and we were gettin' out of there. The rest of us left our stations and went right to our seats. A few minutes later, Chapman came running into the main cabin yelling about 'Man overboard.' The SIC said that the flare was ready to breach and we took off with Chapman and Brown looking like they'd seen death, you know?"

Wentworth's face reflected his anger at Lucas' choice of words.

"Sorry, man. Looking scared, right? And both of them were pretty beat up. Chapman's lip was split and Brown wasn't walking too good. The Captain called each of them to the cockpit separately after we took off and talked to them for about two minutes each, with the cockpit security door shut."

"Then the Captain came on the PA and gave a preview of his debrief for the General. I could tell by the other trainees' expressions that I wasn't the only one who didn't know what to think of that. It was like he wanted to make sure the crew knew that we didn't have a choice in leaving them behind. Seemed like a weird thing to do under the circumstances, but I'm just a slug trainee, so who am I to question?

We got back, the General called for me, asked me if I heard of anyone planning to go AWOL. He reminded me that the Dwellers are inferior to us, that we were selected for our "preeminence." He gave me a little speech like we got at indoc about the Dwellers being less intelligent and how they're content to remain in the only environment they had ever known, blah, blah, blah. Just like the Captain's speech, it felt like a sales job. Meantime, we got two men unaccounted for, maybe hurt, maybe in trouble, we're leaving them for dead, but there aren't bodies--" Lucas realized that he had said too much.

"You better not repeat any of this to anybody. I'll never admit I talked to you—hell, you're a ghost anyway. Truth is, I don't know anything for sure and I don't get paid to think, so forget everything I said."

"I'm not going tell anyone you talked to me. I trust you to keep your mouth shut that Mead and I switched places. I've got more to lose than you do. Can I ask you one more question?"

Lucas stood and waited.

"How close were you to the flare?"

"About five thousand feet above it. We were long gone by the time it blew. Even with the detection equipment we have on board, you still can't calculate the exact moment it's gonna blow."

"That's good. He had time." Wentworth turned to leave the locker room.

"Hey, you can't go into the passageway 'til we're gone, man. Get back in the stall."

Wentworth couldn't think of a better place to go to try to fit the newly gained pieces of information into the big picture. He locked the door behind him.

CHAPTER TWELVE

Jonas, Ellie, and Mark sat at the family dining table once the kids were asleep for the night. Mark wondered if the well-worn top had ever been coated with stain. The spindly legs no longer matched each other in height, but the humble table still served as a good catalyst for meaningful conversation.

"The Plan is perfect, Mark. We have to trust in that. I've witnessed it work a trillion times. To tamper with the Plan is to risk your own existence and possibly hers as well," Jonas said.

"You have made your desire clear to The Spirit and He wants you to be happy and rewarded, Mark. He will not forsake you," Ellie added.

"I'm happy here. I feel like I can do some good here; but I'm frustrated because I'm afraid that if I'm not actively looking for her, she could be slipping farther away from me. Every decision we both make could be moving us farther from each other. There could be an accident or an illness that ends this lifetime, taking us to another Tier. Is it possible for me to get really far behind her or too far ahead of her?"

"That's where the trust comes in. You have to believe that you are exactly where you are meant to be. We think that our best service to you is to help you accept that you have work to do on your own before you reunite with her in Enlightenment," Ellie said gently.

"But this was a mistake. This wasn't part of the Plan. For us to be separated, I mean. We left Tier Three together. We were supposed to enter Tier Four together . . . I knew that. I could see it." Mark referred to the Power of Attraction. Once a person harnessed the power of love, they could bring their desires into reality. Mark had harnessed that power very early in his Journeys.

Ellie nodded her understanding. "Still, there are gifts that The Spirit cannot bestow on His beloved because He knows what is best for us."

"Bullshit!" Mark said loudly; then he quickly looked over to his shoulder to make sure that he hadn't awakened the children.

Jonas and Ellie didn't chastise him.

"Something took her from me. Something I couldn't see. Actually pulled her from me. As we were departing the Tier, she was taken," Mark explained.

The Knowers stole a glance at each other.

"Did you feel her being pulled away?" Jonas asked.

"I felt it and I saw it. It wasn't a fully formed figure, it was more like . . ." Mark searched for the description.

"A shadow?" Jonas asked, as if he already knew the answer.

"Exactly!" Mark burst out again. This time Sarah stirred.

"Son, there are no mistakes. You have come to us for a very specific reason. We are familiar with shadow people. In fact the most elevated Knower, the one who is more Enlightened than any other Journeyer is here. He led you to us and he will reveal himself to you when the time is right. We must be patient now and focus on the lessons at hand." Jonas got up from the table and held out his hand for Ellie. They lay down on the floor next to their children.

Mark was more frustrated than ever, but he also had hope. He had to be patient.

CHAPTER THIRTEEN

Dean wasn't home, so Mark sat down to wait for him. A baby started to cry nearby--the uncommon sound unlocked his favorite memory of Tier Three.

He was holding her hand. The doctor instructed her to give one final push.

Mark witnessed the miracle through happy tears. The newborn little boy had a strong cry, but quieted instantly when placed in his mother's arms. He nestled as close to her as he could manage.

Mark cradled them both as he focused on the little face that he had waited so long to see. The tiny baby seemed to be a perfect blend of both of them. He had her plump, round lips and a hint of her black hair. His eyes were the same shade of blue that Mark shared with his father and brothers.

Mark shivered at the memory. It was as clear as when he had lived the scene two existences ago. He never had a flashback as strong as this one and he was encouraged that it might mean he was still on her frequency.

"You sit idle more than any employee I've ever had," Dean commented as he walked into to the campsite. "But considering that I don't pay you anything, I guess there isn't much I can say about it." He laughed at his own joke.

"I was waiting for you," Mark said defensively. "And I don't have anything to work on--we're at a standstill."

"Not anymore!" Dean's eyes sparkled with the excitement. The older man's dirty beard lifted a full two inches when he smiled.

Mark liked the smile in spite of the fact that it revealed missing teeth and the fact that Dean hadn't owned a toothbrush in a long time.

"I found the rubber!"

"No kidding? Let me see it," Mark had been resting on an overturned barrel and he stood up to see what Dean was removing from his worn shoulder bag.

The piece of rubber was old and cracked, yet thick and soft enough to do the job. It was a large piece and would provide two flappers, which completed the collection of parts necessary to make the pump. Mark had found pieces that would work as end caps and Dean knew a recipe to make a waterproof bond—they just had to assemble the pump and a huge part of the filtration system would be finished.

"Who's crazy now, huh?" Dean yelled to his neighbors. They ignored him as usual.

"Let's get started, kid. I'll feel better about not having filters if I have myself a working pump!" Dean said optimistically.

Mark held the pipe to the rubber to determine where he would have to make his incisions while Dean began to make the adhesive.

"So, who was that boy who came to see you the other day?" Mark asked.

Dean looked up from his task with a confused look on his face, "I've never seen him before. I thought he was with you."

CHAPTER FOURTEEN

When Mark and Dean had finished working for the day, Mark decided to walk around the small town to look for the blond boy. He walked slowly down the path where most of the campsites were. He walked back and forth on the street where Jonas's house stood, where the boy had been playing the first time Mark saw him. Mark observed how the Surface Dwellers reacted to him when they saw him coming— they turned and traveled in the opposite direction or avoided his gaze while keeping their distance. He didn't feel comfortable asking any of them about the boy.

While Mark walked, he thought about what might have happened to Lon. He tried to convince himself that Lon may have found a way to contact the battleairship and that it was possible that they returned for him, but he knew that wasn't true. The Army shuttlecraft had a pulse engine that would have been heard for miles if it had returned.

Mark ran into Jonas and John on the path. They walked to where Sarah was babysitting and continued together to the family home. Ellie was waiting for them and she had a room temperature bowl of soaked grain rationed out for each. Mark was thankful for the tasteless nourishment and the few sips of fresh water that washed it down.

Mark updated the family on the progress he and Dean had made on the filtration system. The family was excited and dreamed out loud about having endless clean water for bathing, laundry, and drinking.

When it was time for Sarah and John to go to sleep, the family, including Mark, held hands and said out loud the things that they were thankful for. Mark was thankful for the peaceful atmosphere inside the simple home.

Just as Ellie and Jonas sat down with Mark for another illuminating discussion, there was a knock on the door.

Ellie smiled at Mark, her eyes twinkling, "I believe it's for you," she said to Mark.

The first emotion that gripped Mark was fear. Even though he had been on a loving frequency with this family just a moment ago, he lost control of his mind and reverted to a loveless state.

Possibilities flashed through his mind and he pictured the Surface Dwellers treating him to the harsh welcome they may have given Lon. He pictured soldiers from The World Army coming to arrest him and throw him in the Brig for insubordination aboard the shuttlecraft.

The look on Ellie's face brought him back to reason. She was obviously excited and he was compelled to answer the door without further hesitation.

Mark only had to lean his chair back to reach the knob and let the door swing inward.

The blond haired boy with blue eyes stood in the doorway.

CHAPTER FIFTEEN

The monitor in Wentworth's quarters--really Mark's quarters--came to life and startled Wentworth from his thoughts. A junior trainee was on the screen. Wentworth could tell right away that the kid was full of borrowed authority.

"Mead, you're wanted in General Walther's office, pronto," he snapped. Wentworth was surprised that the monitor silence was being broken and he was personally offended that the General had replaced him in his job so quickly.

"I'll be right up."

When the screen went black, Wentworth felt a boulder of anxiety start to grow in his stomach. He had been in the General's presence every day for almost two years. As the General's assistant, he had executed tasks for him, updated him, and was one of only ten trainees who had unlimited access to the General's office. These coveted jobs went to the top trainees--those with the best academic records and the best reports from the soldiers who put them through their paces.

In spite of his physical similarities to Mark and his past successes in posing for him, Wentworth worried that the General would recognize his face and his voice. This time their identity switch could have deadly consequences. He looked around Mark's room for some sort of camouflage or prop that would help hide his identity.

Wentworth had been through Mead's drawers and his closet several times already. He was surprised by Mark's lack of personal possessions. He had no pictures of his parents or any civilian clothes for his downtime. He didn't own music or books. All he had to his name was Army regulation stuff that had been issued when he came aboard the battleairship. At school, Mark had bunked in a different dorm than the one Wentworth had been assigned to, so he never had knowledge of his friend's private space before.

Wentworth looked critically in the mirror. He didn't remember what color eyes Mark had and they had been friends since childhood, so he didn't think his common brown eyes would tip off the General. He was comforted by the fact that the General had rarely talked one-on-one with Mark and that he was always distracted when he was forced to waste time on trainees. But the mole that Wentworth had by his left ear was a distinguishing trait that the General might remember. The trainee uniform came complete with a hat that no one ever wore, but Wentworth put it on now. He pulled it over his ears, which was not regulation, but it hid the mole.

He planned to look down as often as he could to hide the color of his eyes. He was thankful that a full beard had covered Mark's face a few days ago when he had last been to the bridge.

Wentworth didn't want to keep Walthers waiting and each passing second caused the boulder to expand, so he stopped thinking and started moving.

"Mead to see General Walthers," he told the Sergeant in the General's outer office.

"He's expecting you."

Wentworth was relieved to see that the General had a file open on his desk and was too absorbed in it to look up when he walked in.

"That bag over there is the contents of Wentworth's quarters. He bequeathed everything to you in the event that anything should happen to him, so take it and go," the General ordered.

"Yes, sir. Thank you, Sir," Wentworth mumbled to disguise his voice.

He picked up the large bag and was glad to have access to his things again. He threw the sack over his shoulder and opened the door to leave the office.

"Mead," the General barked.

"Yes, sir?" Wentworth kept his back to his superior and began to rehearse how he would answer questions about whether his friend had ever discussed going AWOL.

"I'm glad to see you took our last conversation seriously and shaved off all of that unsanitary facial hair."

"Yes, sir," Wentworth replied, and then raced out the door, slamming it a little too forcefully behind him.

He hurried back to Mark's room and laid all of his possessions on the bed. He was happy to have his things back, especially his hand held tablet. He powered it up and unlocked it. When a trainee got transferred to a new department, everyone in the General's office was given a new password so that access was only available to current office staff. He typed in the password for the General's trainees—thankfully, it still worked. Wentworth guessed that no one had thought to change it because they assumed he wouldn't be attempting to access the database from the Surface.

Wentworth knew that several trainees would be logging and in and out at this time of day and that his doing so wouldn't raise any red flags. He looked for the report of the last mission to the Surface.

He read quickly, as if he could get discovered at any moment, while mumbling under his breath, "Don't get caught, don't get caught, don't get caught . . ."

The official report was nothing like what Wentworth had been told.

General Walther's report stated that, while half of the cargo team was distracted by an accident that occurred while offloading supplies, the other two trainees deserted their posts, their mission, and their loyalties to the World Army. Wentworth and Walker were officially classified as Absent Without Leave.

There was no evidence in the report to support the conclusion of defection.

The document also contained Wentworth's complete record and Walker's file. Since being recruited, Lon Walker had never caused problems or failed to meet expectations. He got good grades, was never written up by his commanding officers, and was a legacy World Army candidate. His father was WA retired. There were no red flags to indicate that Walker would instigate deserting.

Wentworth scanned the correspondence from the General's office for the days following the incident, but the disappearance of the trainees was never mentioned again.

He typed *"Surface incidents"* into the log's search field and found a report of an unnamed region where some Dwellers had started collecting materials to make weapons. When questioned, they said they were planning to roam outside of their territory to see if there were any animals left to hunt. The Army made an example of the town by punishing them severely. The battleairship patrolling their region didn't drop food there for two solid months, until a snitch told them where the remaining supplies were. They started delivering again only after the materials were surrendered. Wentworth remembered learning about the incident in one of his 100 level classes, but felt it wasn't relevant to the Surface event involving Mark.

Satisfied that he was up-to-date on the General's log, Wentworth shut down his tablet and contemplated the information he had just learned.

In the time that Wentworth had been with the WA, they had never lost a soldier. In training class, the instructors used stories of accidents, skirmishes, and dishonorable discharges to prevent history from repeating itself. Wentworth didn't remember being told of any particular rite of passage for soldiers who died while in service to the WA, but it seemed that ignoring it couldn't possibly be protocol. Of course, there was no evidence that Mark and Walker were dead—the mere thought made Wentworth's heart palpitate. He took comfort in Lucas's account of the story, which gave Mark enough time to survive the flare.

It made Wentworth feel disposable to know that the World Army could lose two trainees and, except for the General's egotistical reaction, there was minimal disruption of daily procedures.

Wentworth knew there something sketchy about how the incident was being handled. Of course, nothing like this had ever happened before, so he had nothing to compare it to and there were no guidelines for how to handle a defection. No one had ever defected. Wentworth didn't think Mark and Walker had planned to be the first.

General Walthers should have sent the shuttlecraft back for Mark and Lon, or their bodies. He should have held services to honor the fallen soldiers, should have done almost anything other than what he did. Wentworth vowed to keep digging.

CHAPTER SIXTEEN
REMEMBERING TIER THREE

The waves crashed the shoreline, pounding the beach into smooth submission. Mark sat in the sand and she leaned back against him. Cheek to cheek, both pair of eyes followed their son as he chased the waves back to where they started.

"You'll get the next one, buddy!" Mark called after him.

"Why can't I catch one?" The little boy ran to where his parents were sitting.

"Because the waves are part of the ocean," his mother explained softly. "The waves like to explore, and cool our toes, but the waves belong to the ocean and they can't be separated."

"So, they're like the kids and the ocean is like the parents?" he asked, his eyes wide.

"Yup. Can't be separated," Mark confirmed.

"So when I grow up and get married, can my wife and I live with you and Mom?"

"Of course!"

"So why don't we live with Grandpa and Grandma Mead?" The logical question made his parents laugh.

"Because Grandpa and Grandma Mead travel the world helping people who are sick and they build houses for the poor," she explained.

"I don't wanna travel the world. I like it here," the young boy said.

"Look, the sun is going to bed." Mark pointed to the horizon. The sky exploded into vibrant shades of purple, pink, and orange. The air smelled of plumeria and the breeze caressed their faces.

"The magic never fades, does it?" she whispered reverently.

"And it never will," Mark added.

"The sun is magic?" the boy asked.

"When you meet the girl that you want to spend eternity with, you'll understand all about magic, Marcus," Mark promised.

"I think I already know some grown-up things, Daddy," Marcus said seriously.

"You are pretty smart, Mister, but I have a few more years of experience than you do."

"How old are you, Daddy?"

"Twenty-eight trips around the sun. Ten of those were with your mom and four with you," Mark answered.

"You're OLD!" Marcus' mood turned to awe.

Mark laughed with her and they pulled their little boy into a four-armed hug.

"We have a few more trips around the sun before the waves and the oceans are separated," the little boy said solemnly.

CHAPTER SEVENTEEN

The little blond boy with the blue eyes entered the house quietly and smiled at the sight of the children cuddled peacefully in the corner.

"Mark, we told you that there are other Knowers here. This is Adam. He is the most enlightened Knower currently on this Tier," Jonas explained.

"Hi, Adam," Mark shook hands with the boy.

"Peace," the boy replied.

"We asked Adam to come help us explain what you need to know. Jonas and I don't want to tell you more than what should be revealed to you, yet we want give you enough information to help you make a good decision about what you are up against," Ellie told Mark.

"Okay," Mark said tentatively. "Anything you can tell me about how to find my lost soul mate would be incredible. And if I could find the soul we created, I would be grateful."

"I know your story, Mark. I know what happened," Adam said.

Mark nodded to encourage the little boy to keep talking.

"Do you know about Shadows, Mark?"

"Probably not," Mark guessed.

"When you reach a certain stage in your Journeys, and it happens at different times for each soul, you will be able to shadow yourself," Adam began.

"Many reach Enlightenment without ever knowing that such a possibility exists. Very few ever need the skill and most who discover it use it as a tool for revenge, manipulation, or sabotage. Shadowing is a risk that many unwittingly take because they were never told how dangerous it is. That is why I am telling you this now, Mark. Someone here will tempt you to solve your problems by shadowing without telling you the risks."

"The possible benefit to shadowing is that you can send a shadow of yourself, capable of all the things your true self is capable of, to travel to another Tier. It is impossible for the full soul to do that, as you know, unless The Spirit approves the desire. Your shadow can only visit or revisit Tiers that would not contain lessons for you, Tiers that are beneath your level of development. Your shadow cannot go ahead of you in your Journey. The risk is, being that the travel between levels is not authorized, the shadow may not make it back to your full soul. If something happens to your shadow on another Tier, your soul is forever compromised and you will not reach Enlightenment. You will be stuck forever in the existence that you sent the shadow out from." Adam raised his eyebrows to question whether Mark had understood everything so far.

Mark nodded for Adam to continue.

"You have probably met people during your Journeys that were shadowless souls. We see them as deranged, mentally incapable, severely physically disabled, or worse."

Mark heard the second part of Adam's explanation, but was more interested in the first part. "You said that these shadows can travel to other Tiers and they can come back to the soul. Can a shadow bring a full soul with it? Or two full souls?"

"The Spirit has no law about this. To allow a shadow of your soul to travel outside of the soul is not part of the Design. It evolved through free will. It is done without the guidance of The Spirit. Everything that we do throughout our Journeys is done with Him. He is constantly intervening in our experiences. Challenging us when we need it or making things easier when the burden is too heavy. But when you travel outside of the laws, you're on your own. You cannot invoke Him. That is why shadow travelers are very secretive about what they do. I know of souls who have successfully traveled and returned back. They go for many reasons, from making amends to causing trouble. But I have never heard of someone bringing back a full soul," Adam said.

"Let alone two souls," Mark added wearily.

"I have good news about the second soul that you seek. The one you knew as your child on Tier Three is in this realm, but in grave danger of not completing the Journey. He has chosen death over life. He does not seek Enlightenment."

Mark stood up from the table, "Can you take me to him?"

"Sit down, Mark," Jonas said. There is still far more to tell you."

CHAPTER EIGHTEEN

Wentworth discovered that Mark's daily duties in the machine shop weren't as easy as they looked. Mark fixed broken mechanical items and salvaged the parts of useless things to create something new. Wentworth found out that the engineers sometimes came to the shop to ask Mark's opinion—lately "Mark" had been uncharacteristically inept at solving puzzling mechanical glitches. Wentworth wasn't as good as Mark was at making old space heaters into desk lamps, but the time spent tinkering gave him time to think and he enjoyed the solitude of the work.

Life aboard the ship had gotten back to normal. The curfew was lifted, talking was allowed again, and the communication monitors were in full service. Still, the World Army had made no official statement about what happened to the two missing trainees.

Wentworth decided that he needed to network and copping Mark's personality was a good way to do it. Wentworth decided to host a poker game that would feature more drink than cards. He figured if he could get guys together in a safe place, their egos would force them to compete to see who knew the most about the ill-fated supply drop.

He knew that Mark's close friends would know right away that Wentworth was impersonating Mead, so he invited guys that Mark didn't know too well and included names of trainees who had been on the shuttle during the supply drop.

Wentworth, having been the one to write up the disciplinary reports for the General, knew where to go to get drink—the laundry room. He asked ten guys to come to his room at eleven that night, but to keep it quiet.

Wentworth attended Mark's parties, so he planned to host the way Mark would. It would be easy to play the type of music Mark would have chosen—Wentworth's digital music player was loaded with the playlists Mark created when he borrowed the device. After stealing some snacks from the Mess, Wentworth taught himself to play poker from a tutorial on his tablet. He was more comfortable being the guy sitting in the corner at parties than he was being the center of attention. Taking Mark's place as the host and dealer made him nervous.

The day dragged, but at eleven the soft taps on his stateroom door came one after another. The guys filled every inch of the small cabin, but they were so used to being cramped that they barely noticed.

Wentworth dealt hand after hand and once everyone had downed a few drinks and loosened up, he asked the question of the night. "So, have you guys heard any more about Wentworth and Walker?"

"Yeah, man. Some crazy stuff went down on that shuttle." Wentworth detected an accent heard in the perimeter regions.

"Like what?" Wentworth asked casually.

"They were thrown overboard, dude. There was a big fight and Chapman and Brown literally threw them out the hatch." The guy who was talking paused after each of his last three words for effect. "I fold." He laid his cards face down on the table.

"Call--I heard that too," Wentworth baited him. "You know why? You think they were told to do it?"

"Nah, man that would be too cold. And why would anyone try to off Wentworth? He was like the General's bitch or something, wasn't he?"

"He worked in the office along with nine other guys," Wentworth said defensively.

"Sorry, Mark," the kid replied. "I forgot you went to school with him. He was your buddy, right?"

"Yeah."

"I heard you got his stuff," another trainee said. "Raise."

"I fold--Where did you hear that?" Wentworth asked.

"I'm raising, baby. A couple guys in the office. They said that the General gave his stuff to you 'cuz Wentworth filled out the papers, but they threw Walker's things in the incinerator. He talked about his Mom, so I know he had a next-of-kin. I don't think they even tried to get word to her."

"General's probably got someone watching her to see if Lon turns up by her," someone scoffed. "Fold—I don't have big pimp money like you guys."

"Wentworth is not the type to go AWOL, but I didn't know Walker. Did he want to go back to the Surface?" Wentworth asked as he dealt the river.

"Naw, no way. He was a lifer," said the guy with the accent. "I'm gonna raise."

"It's like the soldiers and the General want to ignore that Walker and Wentworth ever existed. Makes you think that if we ever get called to service, we all just have numbers on our backs."

"Yeah, man. At first I thought the curfew and imposing silence on the ship was out of respect for the fallen, but after a while it felt more like a punishment. And the Information Officer never used their names. The only reason we know who went MIA is 'cuz we were there. I know we're just trainees, but there should be respect for future soldiers who were dedicating themselves to keeping world peace."

"If you think we got punished, be glad you're not on the Surface in that region right now. I hear we aren't dropping food where Wentworth and Walker went overboard for a month. The General thinks that they went AWOL and had help from the Dwellers to do it."

One of the poker players let out a low whistle.

"Betting's capped." Wentworth moved the game along and wanted to make sure he had everyone's attention so that he could make a point. "If they got thrown overboard, the Dwellers are getting punished for something they didn't do and the WA just left our guys for dead."

"Do you think they're dead?" One of the guys asked quietly.

"If the flare didn't burn 'em up, I bet the Dwellers killed 'em. You know what it's like to be desperate. The Dwellers would've seen their clothes and wondered what they were carrying. That's reason enough to kill down there," someone slurred.

Suddenly, Wentworth had as much of the conversation as he could stand. "Enough about that. I don't wanna talk about it anymore," he said. "Show what you got."

"Kinda hard to move on when we keep circling the region. We've been at ten thousand feet and in the same pattern since it happened," one of the guys volunteered.

"How do you know that? They don't share the flight plan with trainees," someone challenged.

"I work on the flight deck. They're teaching me navigation," he replied. "And it looks like I get the pot! Suck on that!"

Wentworth gathered the cards for another hand. He hadn't won any money, but he had acquired some useful information. He knew there would only be one reason for the battleairship to stay in a region where they had no intention of dropping supplies. They were waiting for something.

CHAPTER NINETEEN

An hour after the General's trainees would have begun their daily office work, Wentworth used the password to sign into the network. Although he had committed much of the information to memory, he felt compelled to reread everything related to the Surface mission in case he missed something. He looked up Lon's file and immediately received an error message:

File Not Found.

Wentworth rapidly tapped his fingers against his lips while he absorbed the information. He typed his own name in the search.

File not Found.

He located Mark's file and scanned it for any information that might assist him in maintaining his false identity. Nothing jumped out at him that he hadn't already known. He went all the way back to Mark's enlistment paperwork. Mark had named Wentworth as his next of kin and made provisions for him to inherit his belongings should anything happen to him. Wentworth was touched that Mark had made the same choice that he had—they had never discussed it. Knowing how little Mark actually had made it seem less of a big deal though. Neither of them had a functional family. The school had been the only family they really knew . . . which made the information from the next line so interesting. The Guidance Counselor at the school had encouraged both boys to take the admissions test for the World Army. The Counselor granted Wentworth permission to enlist in Army Training. The person listed as the guardian giving consent for Mark was Garrison Walthers. On the battleairship, everyone called Garrison Walthers The General.

CHAPTER TWENTY

Mark enjoyed working with Dean, but today it felt like a waste of time. The soul he had created with his love was in this realm and Mark wanted to be searching for him. Adam had convinced Mark that it was important to maintain his daily routine. Mark's Plan was perfect and his daily life, even the most mundane task, was designed to produce miracles.

Dean's high-pitched voice distracted Mark from his thoughts.

"Look-y, this will be a perfect natural filter, won't it?" Dean showed his find to Mark.

The material was soft, grainy, and pure. It was readily available on the Surface, didn't dissolve in water, and was packed closely together.

"There's only one way to find out." Mark helped Dean pour the filtering material into the area of the system they referred to as "Center Stage." Dean started the pump.

The process was excruciatingly slow, but both men watched intently as the murky water became clear in only half a day's time.

As the water dripped into the "sterile" aluminum buckets, Dean could barely contain himself.

"That's a dream coming true, son! Right there! Years and years of thinking it, and here it's happening before my eyes!" Dean danced around and whooped wildly.

Mark couldn't help but be amused and he was proud that he had helped Dean accomplish the important task.

"Dance with me, son! Don't they let you dance in the Army?" Dean pulled on Mark's hand to try to lift the much heavier young man to his feet.

Mark laughed and remembered what it felt like to be drunk. It was a lot like this—doing whatever made sense to you at a time when you were oversaturated. In this case, he was soaked with joy.

Mark stood up and imitated Dean's whoop. "Try this old man!" Mark showed his worst attempt at dancing.

By the time the supposed sun was directly overhead, the pair had filtered three barrels of water and had so much refreshed water that they didn't have adequate storage for it. They had to give it away. Neighbors in the town were hysterical with gratitude and gave Dean the credit that he had always dreamed of attaining.

"You know, this system doesn't remove viruses," Mark whispered to him. "It isn't completely clean. We can't really measure the purity of it."

"Look at it. It's pure. Taste it! It tastes better than that chemically enhanced garbage they give us from the battleairship. The proof is right here." Dean beamed.

The townspeople had gathered together after hearing that Dean's water filtration machine worked and that free samples were being handed out. Mark filled a large container with pure water--water that had been thick muck when the sun first shone on it that morning.

"Old man, I'm going to let you disperse your treasure as you see fit. If it's okay with you, I'm going to take some back to Jonas's house," Mark said.

"Take a barrel-full! I got plenty!" Dean shouted.

On the road back, several townies smiled at Mark. Others spoke to him for the first time, thanking him for his efforts. Some still avoided his eyes, not convinced that the "fresh" water wasn't some kind of manipulation that the Army was perpetrating.

Mark found Ellie at home. She jumped to her feet as soon as the door opened.

"Were you lying down?" Mark asked her. "Please, go back to sleep. I'm just delivering cleaned water. If you have the rare chance at some privacy, I'll go walking."

Mark was anxious to embark on locating his son.

"No, Mark, it's okay. Please stay," Ellie replied.

Mark tried to mask his disappointment.

"It isn't like you to be home in the middle of the day. Is everything okay?"

"No. I haven't been okay for a while. For the sake of the kids, Jonas and I have agreed not to let on. Even Knowers have limits on how long they may reside on a Tier," Ellie said softly.

"So," Mark looked at her bald head and swallowed hard. "So, the story the kids told me about trading your hair for water . . ."

Ellie smiled. "We told them that so they wouldn't worry. Who needs hair when the fundamentals of life are so scarce?"

"Vanity is one of the greatest weaknesses of humans," Mark said. "I wasn't surprised to hear that someone would trade life-sustaining water for hair to make a wig."

"I'm sick. We don't know how sick, but my energy level is low. I have been sitting with dying people for so long now that I see the stages. My skin is getting thin, my fingernails don't grow, my eyes are yellowing . . . I don't think I will be here this time next year," Ellie said.

"The children . . ." Mark shook his head.

"They will be fine. Jonas will guide them through their Journey. They will miss me, of course, but I will be with them again in Enlightenment. I only hope that my love was strong enough for them to remember me."

"Of course it is!" Mark assured her. "You love them with every fiber of your being, Ellie. Of course they feel that."

"It isn't how much I love them that determines whether the love will last. What matters most is if they let the love reside in their hearts. Sometimes even the strongest love is forgotten."

Mark understood what she was hinting at. "She felt the same way I did, Ellie. We belonged to each other so much that we were the same person."

Ellie smiled at the thought.

"I'm so sorry for what you're going through." Mark poured her a large class of clean water. "Maybe this will help you feel better for the moment. Dean and I are in the business of giving away filtered water."

"The filtration system works?" Ellie asked.

"Well, there is no way to test the quality of it, but it looks good and tastes good," Mark handed her the glass.

"Thank you, Mark."

"I'm going to go out and give you some more time to rest before the kids come home looking for dinner. And now that I know, you can count on me to help out a lot more around here," Mark told her. "And I won't let on to the kids."

"When the time is right, we'll tell them. Thank you for your discretion." Ellie finished the glass of water in a few sips. "The water is wonderful."

Mark closed the door behind him and decided to explore the empty town. Everyone was at Dean's. Mark hadn't had the opportunity to properly survey the Surface since he arrived and it had been nearly two years since he was able to walk for a long stretch outdoors.

As he walked, he surrounded the town with love. Mark had learned that when he actively loved the people and the things round him, the surrounding energy changed. Sometimes, if he concentrated hard enough, the person or thing receiving love radiated with a warm, golden hue. In his mind, he surrounded Ellie with love in the hope that it would make her stronger. Mark thought of his son and waited for a telltale glow that might reflect his love, but there was no reciprocal energy coming back at him.

There were a few camps outside of town. They looked as if they had been abandoned, but the populated town gave the same impression. As Mark walked, the terrain remained the same. As far as the eye could see, red-brown dirt covered everything. Even the water sources were the same russet color, but Mark felt proud to have contributed to making that water usable for the Dwellers.

During his time on the battleairship, Mark had forgotten about the smell of the Surface. Pungent sulfur dominated the scene. Mark's school was far from where he was now, but the odor there was exactly the same. He imagined that the entire planet was shrouded in the same putrid stench.

The supposed sun hung in the blurred sky. The dirt from the Surface was inescapable. It collected in Mark's nostrils and coated his eyelashes. It was suspended in the still air and, when Mark squinted, almost made the Surface look beautiful through its soft focus. Almost. This land wasn't fit for living beings. The animals had died off long ago—the humans were more adaptable and more stubborn. As far back as the histories went, the Surface had been this way and Mark often wondered if anything better could ever be cultivated from this world of dirt.

Mark loved the freedom of being able to walk a great distance in any direction. The safety and comfort of his residence on the battleairship came with logistical restrictions. On the ship, he ran a thousand feet on a straight away, then turned with the curve of the bow to run another thousand feet and turned again at the stern.

The young GI saw the same gray walls everyday on the ship. They were polished to a shine and there was always a fragrance of a cleaning agent in the air. In their own way, cleanliness and sterility had a type of beauty; but to Mark, nothing could replace being unrestricted.

He walked until his feet hurt, then headed back to the house. He wanted to get home before anyone else so that he could make the dinner and allow Ellie to rest a bit longer, but he was the last to arrive.

When Mark opened the door, the house was full. Jonas, John, Ellie, and Sarah sat around the table behind four mismatched cups brimming with water.

"What are you doing home so early?" Mark asked Jonas.

"John and I have been given a half day off to celebrate the new water filtration system. The seniors found out that the engineer behind the breakthrough lived with us, so we were rewarded," Jonas explained. "The filter changes life for the people in this region, Mark. None of the water we carry is for the town; it only powers the generators."

Mark hadn't noticed any electrical power in the town. "What do the generators run?" He asked.

"Our communication center. It's what keeps us connected to the other regions. You were fortunate to get stranded in the richest and most advanced civilization on the Surface!"

Mark nearly burst out laughing, but successfully stifled himself when he realized that Jonas was serious.

"You knew about the generators and what they power?" Mark asked the kids.

They nodded slyly in reply. "We weren't going to tell an Army Trainee about our communication center." John explained. "We're young, not dumb."

Mark smiled. "But what does the filtered water Dean and I made have to do with running the generators? Our water is going to be used to keep people alive and clean. Maybe we'll even figure out a way to make this dirt yield some crops, now that we can irrigate."

Jonas raised his eyebrows. "You sound like an independent man now. Independent men are difficult to control," Jonas said. "Having our own resource for water and having a communication center are important steps towards establishing our self-sufficiency."

"So, your region is planning to revolt against the World Army?" Mark asked.

"We prefer to say that we are preparing to declare our independence from the World Army," Ellie smiled. "That way we don't have to worry about eating their population-controlling food and drinking their tainted water."

Mark asked Ellie the question with his eyes.

She nodded her reply.

The World Army was playing God with the Surface Dwellers.

CHAPTER TWENTY-ONE

Wentworth was not a great lover of conspiracy theories. When his fellow students at the Surface school blamed the World Army for the conditions that the Dwellers lived in, Wentworth tuned out. His attitude was that some things just are the way they are. Sometimes things suck and sometimes you can find a lot to be happy about. Even in the worst of times, like when he lost his family, Wentworth felt comforted by his classmates and the teachers who did their best to make him feel secure.

At the school, they encouraged any of the boys who were Army material to enlist as trainees. Those who weren't good candidates were taught skills and trades so that they could contribute to their regions when they completed the school curriculum. Few Dwellers had any sort of education so skilled workers on the Surface were indispensable. To Wentworth, these efforts made by the World Army to care for the Dwellers' orphans forgave any collateral damage they inadvertently caused along the way. The Army didn't have to fund schools—they could have let the Dwellers' take care of their own. Overall, Wentworth thought the Army did a pretty good job of providing for the Dwellers while maintaining order.

He had worked hard in school to build an impressive academic record and he displayed self-discipline with the hope that he would be singled out for military service. Wentworth had his future mapped out— he would serve in the World Army until retirement then settle in one of the Army's Surface regions. He would live in military housing and provide his child, if he had one, the same education he received in the military school.

Wentworth chose to turn a blind eye to the fact that Mark's recruitment blasted his theory that the Army was looking for the best and the brightest candidates. Mark was a cool guy. He made friends easily, enjoyed life, and didn't care too much about rules. He worried when it was appropriate, but rebounded to his typical positive attitude quickly. He went out of his way to help anyone who needed it, to listen to someone who needed to talk, or to encourage anyone who felt defeated. He was a great friend/brother. But Mark wasn't a good student. He was well liked by his teachers, even though he often left his homework and his chores until the last minute and had to be reminded. The school sought to build independence, but Mark practiced the type of independence that required assistance.

Wentworth knew from working in the General's office that most trainees had records like his own or they had a rare, unique affinity for something useful. As glad as Wentworth was that they had both been selected as Army recruits, he couldn't understand how Mark got accepted as a trainee. Wentworth knew that Armies required different types of men and he liked to think that he was being groomed to be an Officer. Maybe Mark was destined to retire as a soldier.

Wentworth was reconsidering his former mind-set in light of recent developments. Protocol was being followed selectively after the loss of two trainees only assumed to be dead. The fact that neither one had been confirmed deceased didn't seem to bother anybody. The "No Man Left Behind" rule had been broken. The battleairship was no longer patrolling its territory and the Dwellers were being punished for an event that they couldn't possibly have caused. If there was ever a time to entertain conspiracy theories, Wentworth knew it was now.

He needed unlimited access to the General's database and all communications on the battleairship. Wentworth could tap in by syncing his tablet with the server, allowing him to remotely access the information. He knew that it was possible, but he had to make sure that his unauthorized access wasn't discovered. He needed help doing that and he knew where to find it.

*　　*　　*　　*

The hacker worked out of the ship's laundry room. He demanded Wentworth's personal music player as a fee. Wentworth handed it over. Within two minutes, his tablet not only had untraceable access to the ship's database and communications, but he also received notifications of activity on the network.

"That took you two minutes. I saved for nearly a year to buy that music player," Wentworth complained.

"You wanted a job done and you asked for me to forget I did it once it was complete," the hacker reminded him. "And it took me years to learn how to do that in two minutes."

"Just give me the damn tablet," Wentworth huffed.

"You're welcome, Mead." The hacker popped the wireless buds into his ears and pressed "Play".

CHAPTER TWENTY-TWO
REMEMBERING TIER THREE

"How do you know that you love me?" She asked, as she rested her head on his chest.

"Say my name and keep your ear pressed right where it is," he replied.

She giggled.

"Go ahead . . . say my name."

"Mark Mead."

His heart responded by quickening its pace.

"How did you do that?" She lifted her head from his chest and pressed her nose to his.

"I have no control over it, but it does that every time you enter a room, say my name, toss your hair, or bake a cake. It just does that all the time when you're around. I react to every physical and emotional signal that you send out," Mark told her.

"What if I got mangled in a terrible accident that disfigured me?" She challenged.

"I love who you are, not how you look."

"You don't love how I look?" she teased him.

"I also love how you look."

"I knew that I loved you the first day we met on the beach," she told him. "I felt you arrive that day. When I saw you for the first time, I said to myself, *'There he is.'* What a relief that you turned out to be a thoughtful, compassionate, and brilliant man." She kissed the tip of his nose.

"I'm brilliant, now?"

"You are brilliant. You are wise and insightful and you don't get distracted by unimportant things," she explained. "I can always count on you to have the right perspective."

"Nothing that we face is difficult as long as we're together. As long as you and Marcus are happy, healthy, and safe, life is beautiful. And I will do everything in my power to make sure it stays that way."

"Do you think that love is the strongest thing in the universe?" she asked.

"It is. Don't doubt that," he told her. "I just gave you incontrovertible proof."

"I love you, Mark. You are the half of myself that I like best." She softly kissed his lips.

"I don't know what amazing thing I did in another life to deserve you, but I must have been all the things back then that you think I am now."

She giggled again, "Please kiss me and never stop."

Mark did as he was told.

CHAPTER TWENTY-THREE

Lon saw the heap on the Surface dust. From a distance, he thought it might be some lost clothing or pieces of cloth that fell from a wanderer's sack; but as he got closer, he could see that it was a person. Lon approached the body quietly. It was a powerful-looking man dressed in worn, tattered clothing. Lon's internal alarm bells were going off. Something wasn't right—no wanderer would lie down alone and unprotected in the middle of the day.

Lon gently kicked the guy's elbow. There was no movement. He nudged the vulnerable head with the toe of his boot. No reaction. Lon kicked a little harder—still nothing. When he bent down to search through the guy's pockets the corpse came to life, attacked Lon, and had him on his back with a knife to his throat before Lon knew what happened.

"Identify yourself!" The man shouted in Lon's face. Then he relaxed his grip. "Oh, it's you."

CHAPTER TWENTY-FOUR

Dean's campsite was mobbed with people. They were waiting in line, celebrating, and marveling.

"Production is up fifty percent from yesterday," Dean bragged to Mark. "I tweaked her a little here and there and I was able to increase the capacity without sacrificing efficiency. Then I had to get people to start making containers to hold all the water!"

Mark slapped Dean on the back, "Your invention is probably the most important thing that has ever happened here."

"I couldn't have done it without you, Mark."

"Not true. You would have figured it out."

"You were a big help to me and I want to show my appreciation." Dean walked away from the mob and gestured for Mark to follow him.

"Do you have anything that you'd like to ask of me? Give me a chance to return the favor you did for me."

"Thanks Dean, but I have everything I need. I thought I was screwed when I got pushed off the shuttlecraft, but I have a place to stay, I have food, I have water." Mark smiled at the older man. "I've made friends. I'm doin' pretty well."

"Your eyes say somethin' different."

Mark laughed. "Well, I'll tell my eyes to shut up, then, because I'm fine."

"The grief, the sorrow, the loss. It's all in there. I can see it. I like to think of myself as an old soul. And having been around a while has taught me a few things about people. You're damaged, Mark. You lost something that once made you complete." Dean didn't put a question mark on the end of his sentence.

"Um . . . Dean, I . . ."

"Do you want my help or not?"

"Help with what?"

"People here think I'm nuts. They think I'm only half there." Dean circled his pointer finger around his temple. "Well you know what? They're right. Most of the time, I'm exactly half here." He spoke more vehemently than Mark had ever heard him.

"So where is the other half of you?" Mark attempted humor to regain control of the conversation.

"Making things right on another Tier, Mark. Just the way you could be doin' right now."

Mark remembered Adam's warning that someone in this realm would attempt to help Mark by teaching him to shadow without considering the risks. He grew increasingly nervous, but there was an excitement in his stomach that he hadn't felt yet in this existence.

111

"I know someone who can teach you to send a clone of yourself to another Tier to correct the thing that caused the sadness in your eyes," Dean whispered.

Mark wanted to find out what he could without getting in too deep. "Let's say you're right--that I do want to travel to another Tier. Let's say I get there and want to come back with another soul from that Tier. Is that possible?"

"I've never heard of that. I'm sure you could send a shadow and live there for a period of time. Once the soul you want to protect, or teach a lesson to, departs that Tier, you can send your shadow back to your soul. Then, you can find the soul again and shadow them in their next existence if you want to."

"How is that an answer?" Mark's disappointment came out as anger. "I can be with her until I lose her again and then repeat the process?"

"She is lost to you now, isn't she? This way you get her back."

"I don't want her back temporarily, I want to be together with her throughout our Journeys as it was meant to be," Mark explained. "I knew it was decided, but we were pulled apart as we left Tier Three."

"How was she taken from you?" Dean asked.

Mark struggled, as he often did, to try to see it clearly. He remembered the boat pitching and rolling. He remembered waves two stories tall rolling so closely together than the boat couldn't right itself as it slid down the backside of the swells. He remembered seeing her comfort their son, singing softly to him as she told him that the boat was built to withstand conditions just like that. He remembered the love that surrounded them. And he remembered fear. Then, he tasted saltwater. He grabbed for their hands, found them and used his strength to stay attached as they were pulled from the harrowing experience. He was in darkness and caught a hint of orange blossom fragrance. *Hold on!* He willed the three of them. They were traveling together as it was meant to be. Mark felt the presence of another person—he couldn't see clearly--he anticipated help. But the force pulled them away and it was impossible for Mark to hold on. Then he was alone. He could never conjure a clear picture of the critical events between holding them with all the power of his love and waking up in the Transformation Tier. The memory was always dark and blurred.

"I don't know, but it was a mistake," Mark explained.

"There are no mistakes," Dean said emphatically. "Sometimes the Plan is changed by outside forces. Evil forces."

"There is no evil. There is only lack of love and inserting love can correct any situation." Mark was surprised at his reply—he wasn't as convinced of his position as he was pretending to be.

"The Plan can change. One event can change the course of your Plan forever. What was meant to be today can be replaced by what will be meant to be tomorrow. If you want to get back to what was originally *meant to be* for you, you have to go back and change the event that caused your Plan to take another route," Dean said slowly.

Mark was silent.

"Our heart's desire is supposed to rule. If we have faith . . . if we stay true to our loving nature . . . blah, blah, blah. Why should we have to accept that those who hurt us will eventually get theirs if we aren't there to witness it? Why should we accept that the new Path is truly '*meant to be?*' Why don't we have any power over our own Paths?" Dean raised his eyebrows and cocked his head slightly to one side.

"Because we are still learning what the Journeys have to teach," Mark answered. "Who am I to know what's right? I can't see the big picture."

"Or is that what The Spirit wants you to believe? Did He ever tell us about shadowing? Did He ever tell us that we have this power? Why not? Is it because He wants us on our Path?"

"Yeah. He designed our Paths and He has our best interest at heart. He knows what we want, but He also knows what we need." Mark fought to increase his faith.

"You keep believin' that kid. In the meantime, she might reconnect with another soul. You don't even know if she deleted the existence she shared with you. If she did, you would have to reconnect with her all over again."

"It was instantaneous. We were never apart after the first day that we found each other," Mark told him.

"So maybe you had been pulled apart before," Dean thought out loud.

"What do you mean? You think we were together before?"

"When did you start retaining memories? After you met her?"

Mark nodded.

"To connect immediately usually indicates a reconnection. It is possible you were separated before and found each other again," Dean reasoned.

"Then we will find each other--again."

"Unless there is a force keeping you apart. The Plan might be for you to be together now, but there may be forces at work to keep you apart."

"But nothing is stronger than The Spirit. Nothing is stronger than love, so how could that be?"

"Not every soul chooses to be guided through their Journeys by love. Some find it easier to identify with the other side of love," Dean told Mark.

"I don't know . . ."

"Just meet my friend. She can explain it better than I can," Dean urged.

"Okay, but I'm just going to listen to what she has to say. Nothing more."

Dean reached up to slap his young friend on the shoulder. "Come with me."

CHAPTER TWENTY-FIVE

Wentworth told the machine shop supervisor that he was sick and stayed in Mark's quarters with his tablet. It pinged every few seconds when messages were sent within the system. Wentworth hadn't learned anything new from the communications.

Changes were being made to the battleairship's menu. Trainees received praise from their superiors and the commendations were forwarded to the appropriate personnel files.

Wentworth set the tablet on his bed and got up to use the bathroom. While he was in there, he heard a ping. Another alert closely followed the original and two more sounded in rapid succession. That pattern usually indicated a conversation.

Wentworth stayed in the bathroom to brush his teeth. He was in no rush to read the breaking news—his experience with monitoring the system told him that it was probably something as exciting as a mandate for less laundry soap to be used for each load.

Wentworth lay back on the bed and resumed reading the messages. He was immediately intrigued by the new conversation because the Contact Icon said "Unknown User."

Wentworth read, *Filtration system fully operational.*

The reply said, *Excellent work. Congratulations.*

The party on the other side of the conversation wrote: *Proceeding to Step Three.*

A final message followed: *We are encouraged by your success and hope for more progress. Out.*

Wentworth had no idea what to make of the messages. Every other user on the system had an identifier preceding their posts. The parties on both ends of this conversation were anonymous.

Another ping—the General sent an encrypted message. Wentworth hadn't seen one of those before. His new access was worthless if he couldn't read everything on the system.

Wentworth looked through his belongings and grabbed a picture of a blonde model. She was very comfortable posing for the camera without her clothes. He hoped it would cover the hacker's fee.

CHAPTER TWENTY-SIX

"So, who are you?" Lon asked as the man transitioned from attacking him to helping him to his feet.

"Don't ask questions out here. The Dwellers seem like animals, but some have surprising capabilities. Follow me."

"Where are we going?"

"Shut up, Trainee. I'm not going to tell you again."

Lon was in no position to argue.

The two walked across the seemingly featureless landscape. A short distance from where the man had made himself bait, he began to kick at the sand with his boot. A few inches beneath the seemingly solid landscape, he uncovered a handle. He pulled it and revealed a staircase descending below the Surface.

"Hurry up. I don't want to kill one of these stupid Dwellers just because he saw something he shouldn't have." The man gestured for Lon to start moving. "Get going."

The staircase was steep and enveloped in darkness, except for where singular bare bulbs shed weak spheres of light that didn't touch each other.

Lon started counting steps after a while and stopped counting when he hit 100. The staircase ended at a metal door, similar to an airtight bulkhead like those on the battleairship. The man tapped a code on the keypad, placed his right forefinger on the pad and completed a retina scan. The door swung open.

"I found one of them," the man announced to the Private First Class who sat behind the desk at the front of the huge room.

Lon looked around. He was in an outpost of the World Army; the insignias were everywhere. The open room was the size of three battleairships. There were no dividing walls, just weight bearing beams. Sections were created with furniture and by purpose. From where he stood, Lon could see many desks, office equipment and other types of equipment that he couldn't identify. Farther back, it looked like a barracks, complete with cots and lockers. It wasn't luxurious, but, considering its location, it was impressive.

The PFC spoke into a handheld radio. "Sergeant Humphries is back, Sir. He is not empty-handed."

"Send him back."

The PFC nodded at Humphries who motioned for Lon to follow him down the left side of the expanse. There was only one door in the compound and the Sergeant opened it. On the other side, a very plush room looked entirely out of place. It was like stepping through a portal into another universe. Thick carpet covered the floor from wall to wall. Soft couches and chairs were grouped together, and a distinct, appealing aroma hung in the air. Lon had smelled it once before and immediately recognized it as coffee. A large, imposing figure in Army fatigues with four stars pinned to his chest rose from behind an executive desk and addressed his subordinate as he entered the sanctuary.

"Just one, Sergeant?" the General barked.

"Yes, Sir."

"Wait outside. I'll have orders for you in a minute."

"Which one are you?" the General asked Lon.

"Trainee Lon Walker, Sir."

"You went AWOL on the shuttlecraft expedition to bring supplies to the Surface?" General Hilgers asked.

"No, Sir. I was thrown overboard after expressing my belief that more supplies should be offloaded to accommodate the high number of Dwellers. I realize that what I suggested was not consistent with S.O.P., Sir, but I felt our superior officers would agree that the adjustment was justified."

"Explain, Trainee."

Lon told General Hilgers the whole story about how he was thrown off the craft.

"Is Wentworth dead?" the General asked.

"No, Sir," Lon answered quietly.

"Trainee, our creed mandates that we never leave a man behind."

"Yes, Sir."

"So where is Wentworth?"

"I don't know for sure, Sir." Lon closed his eyes to avoid seeing General Hilgers' disgust.

The room was quiet for a moment, which Lon thought was worse than getting yelled at. He wanted to redeem himself in the eyes of the General, but didn't know if the information he held would do that or dig his hole deeper. He decided to divulge what he knew.

"Before I left my fellow trainee with the Surface healer, I checked his pockets to make sure that no World Army property would fall into the hands of the Dwellers. I found Trainee Mark Mead's currency card. I think the person wearing Wentworth's tags was actually Trainee Mead. We use our currency cards a hundred times a day, so I believe a guy's card before his tags. He was injured, but not badly. I thought it was best for me to try to make contact with the battlairship while he healed and then guide the rescue to the town where he stayed. I figured I'd let the Army sort out his identity crisis." Lon braced himself for General Hilger's reaction.

"What do you know about the construction of a filtration facility in town?" General Hilgers asked.

Lon looked confused. "Nothing, Sir."

"You don't know what they're filtering in town? Is it water or some kind of gas--?" General Hilgers tried to lead his witness to the answer.

"I . . . I really don't know," Lon stammered.

"Are the Dwellers planning an uprising against the World Army?"

"I don't know, Sir."

"You have been very helpful, Walker."

General Hilgers called to the Sergeant waiting outside the door.

"Please take Trainee Walker somewhere where you can make him comfortable," General Hilgers ordered the Sergeant.

The General loved his thick, cushy carpeting. He didn't want to stain it.

CHAPTER TWENTY-SEVEN

It cost Wentworth his favorite photograph and his thickest socks, but the hacker was able to deliver.

Safely back in Mead's quarters, Wentworth read the General's reply to the Unknown User's conversation. It said: *Ready the troops on the Surface.*

Wentworth felt a cold chill run through his entire body. The hair on his arms stood at attention and his neck began to sweat.

He had no knowledge of troops on the Surface. It was just a matter of time until he got called to service.

If the first message turned his world upside down, the next encrypted message shook it apart.

Wentworth most likely on your ship. Mead is on the Surface. Walker sentenced to execution.

The message had been sent four minutes ago and there had been no reply.

Wentworth was momentarily paralyzed with fear, but he knew that standing still was a luxury he couldn't afford. He grabbed what he thought he might need and opened the door to Mead's quarters just wide enough to check the passageway. He expected to see the General's Guard coming for him, but it was filled with trainees. He left the room, blended in among them, and went where he knew they would protect him—the ship's laundry.

CHAPTER TWENTY-EIGHT

The woman was far more beautiful than anyone Mark had seen in this existence. Her eyes radiated love from their unusual lavender centers. Her blond hair shone and softly framed her face. Her light peach skin glowed with luminosity and her lips were full, pink, and soft. Dean looked like a monster standing next to her.

"This is the one I have been telling you about," he said to her. "This is Mark."

"Mark, I am Marina," she said smiling, offering her hand.

"It's nice to meet you," Mark replied.

"Thank you for the filtered water," she said to Dean. "I was able to drink my fill and bathe in its pure perfection."

"Anything for you, Marina." Dean turned to Mark. "If it's okay with you, I'll leave you two to talk."

Mark nodded. He didn't feel threatened by this lovely creature.

"Mark, I believe I can help you," Marina told him.

Mark nodded.

"I have helped many before you using the method that my father taught me and his father taught him," she began.

"Your soul has reached a certain strength. Your Journeys have given you experiences that have allowed you to grow. You are close to Enlightenment, but still have much to gain from the experiences before you."

"Are you a Knower?"

"I benefit from the histories passed down. I share knowledge gained by others, not knowledge I personally discovered," Marina answered.

"Have you ever done it yourself?" Mark asked.

"I have sent shadows of my soul to other Tiers. Each trip is deeply personal for every being and I do not ask to know your objectives or reasons for shadowing to another Tier."

"Can you bring a full soul back?"

Marina smiled. "Not without great risk. You must be absolutely certain that you are bringing your soul mate through time and space. If you have connected with your soul mate, the two souls are united as one and, in that case, could travel together as one shadow of one soul."

"And if I successfully brought her here, how would she join this existence?"

"Through you," Marina answered. "She would be a part of you, just as you believe you were joined previously, but, this time, you would share the same vessel. Once here, you would manifest her vessel. If your love is strong enough, you know that you are capable of bringing your desires into being."

"Has it ever been done?"

"I know of a few times, but it depends on your certainty of your soul's counterpart and the strength of your love to manifest that soul in your present existence."

"There is no question about either factor," Mark assured Marina.

"Then there is nothing to fear."

CHAPTER TWENTY-NINE

Lon saw that Sergeant Humphries had changed from his wanderer costume back into his World Army fatigues. The uniform was different from those worn by the officers on the battleairship and Lon took interest in the comparison.

"What are you looking at?" Humphries asked sharply.

"Nothing. Just waiting for you to lead the way," Lon said. As he spoke, his mind registered what his eyes had noticed. He saw that the back of the Sergeant's shirt was untucked—definitely not regulation—and there appeared to be a bulge in the waistband of his pants.

Humphries laughed. "You don't have to worry about getting lost, there's only one way out. Same way we came in." He pointed ahead and to the right. "That way."

When they got to the stairs, Sergeant Humphries directed Lon to take the lead. Lon had thought the worst that could happen to him was a court-martial, but he sensed that something lethal was breathing down his neck. Literally.

As he climbed, Lon devised a plan. He consciously maintained a slow pace in order to conserve the energy he would need. The Sergeant had beaten him in their first wrestling match; but, this time, Lon would have the advantage of a surprise attack.

"So, where are we going?" Lon tried to keep his voice even.

"To another bunker where the Surface based trainees have their quarters. I'll introduce you to the guys and get you set up so you can rest. Only Officers stay in the bunker where General Hilgers' office is."

"Sounds good. I haven't eaten in a while. Is there grub?"

"Of course," Humphries assured him.

When Lon reached the top of the stairs, he pretended that he couldn't lift the exterior hatch. He didn't want the Sergeant at his back. After some pretty good acting, Humphries conceded that Lon must be weak from all the walking he had done without nutrition. The Sergeant lifted the hatch and emerged on the Surface with Lon close behind.

Lon didn't waste a second. He launched himself onto the back of the Sergeant and found his eyes with his fingernails. The man screamed in pain. Lon didn't stop.

Survival was the trophy and, after an exhausting struggle, Lon had won. He emptied Humphries's pockets and took the gun from his waistband. Lon had no doubt that the weapon would have been used against him if he had let his guard down. He dragged the Sergeant as far from the hatch as he could manage. He knew that the next few minutes were critical to his survival. When Humphries didn't return, the Army would start looking for him in a radius around the hatch. Lon knew that he had to put a lot of distance between himself and the underground base--fast.

He sprinted toward the town where he had left Mead. Lon hoped that he was still there and that he could find him before the assassins in World Army fatigues did.

CHAPTER THIRTY

Wentworth explained what he had learned to the only person he felt he could trust--the hacker. The hacker informed other crewmembers who shared his own cynicism about the Army they blindly signed up to serve. Hours later, Wentworth sat in the company of many of the same degenerates that he, as the General's assistant, had reprimanded. These "delinquents" were independent thinkers and didn't swallow every bit of rhetoric the Army fed them. They had come to the same conclusions that Wentworth had. First, the Surface Dwellers were about to be unlawfully attacked by the World Army and, if that wasn't disconcerting enough, a kill had been ordered on a trainee.

There were nineteen trainees assembled in the laundry and each one offered more names for consideration to join their newly formed cause.

"We're going to need some guys inside the General's office," a trainee suggested.

"We have the tablet," Wentworth reminded him. "They don't know that I'm signed onto the network, so we can monitor everything they do."

"At some point we'll need to take control of the Bridge," the hacker told Wentworth impatiently. "We're gonna need guys inside to help give us access."

The realization that extreme action was inevitable landed in Wentworth's stomach. He was starting a mutiny that would be a tactical military mission.

"Right." Wentworth realized that he had already been removed from the front line of the operation. He would be the brains not the brawn; and he would lead from the back. The decision had been made without discussion or debate.   But Wentworth derived satisfaction from assembling those who would know how to derail the Army's attack on the Surface and possibly rescue Mead.

A guy with a distinctive Western accent spoke up. "I know there are some soldiers who think the Army has gone in the wrong direction under the current administration. Lots of guys have family on the Surface and they aren't going to willingly attack without justification. I think we need to go as public with this info as we can."

"Only tell the soldiers and trainees who we know for sure think the way we do," Wentworth cautioned. "We can ask them to meet with us here at midnight."

"If you aren't one hundred percent sure of a guy's loyalty, that's not our guy," the hacker reiterated. "You mention this to the wrong person and not only does it kill the mutiny, but we'll all get strung up."

"Like Lon," a guy from the laundry said softly.

CHAPTER THIRTY-ONE

"You won't be able to sustain the shadow for long on your first try," Marina told Mark.

He contemplated waiting until he had the chance to speak with Adam, Jonas, and Ellie that night, but when he heard that this first trip would likely be a quick test run, Mark couldn't resist giving it a try.

"Teach me how to do it," he begged Marina.

"You must first set your course. Not to *where*, but to *whom*," she instructed. "Feel love for her until you can visualize her standing next to you and you can reach out and touch her."

Mark spent hours every day visualizing her, so he achieved the directive effortlessly.

"Next, will your shadow to leave your soul. This is the harder part because you have never thought of your soul as anything other than a whole."

"Like lifting a layer?" Mark asked, eyes closed.

"If that is what it is like for you, then yes."

"You have to project that layer, that exact replica, complete by itself and yet half of a whole, outside of yourself," Marina coaxed.

Mark pictured his being. He had no idea what his soul looked like, so it was easier to picture his familiar vessel. He pictured one Mark stepping out from the original Mark.

He could see this happening, but he couldn't feel it happening. He focused all the love he had, but still couldn't make his shadow take a step.

"Talk me through it."

"Open your eyes and make your shadow open its eyes. You can't see from the perspective of the shadow with your eyes closed."

Mark opened his eyes and immediately lost the feeling of standing beside her. It was difficult to imagine her when he was in the middle of a reality that seemed genuine.

"Ahhhh!" he yelled in exasperation.

"So, you expected to execute on the first try?"

"You said it would be a short trip, so yeah, I thought that meant I could take a short trip," Mark snapped.

Marina smiled. "It's like walking for the first time. It will take practice and many failed attempts."

"Good to know. So, let's get back to it. I start by visualizing her here . . ." Mark tried to see her beside him, holding hands with him, smiling at Marina. He got that far, and then concentrated on making it feel real. He was thankful for having her there with him. He remembered how she always smelled like soap and orange blossoms. He remembered how, when he would squeeze her hand, she wouldn't miss a beat squeezing back.

Mark focused. After a few minutes, she was still there. He gave more love to her image and increased the gratitude he felt for being next to her again.

Mark tried to hold that feeling in his mind while he peeled his soul in half. He could feel the shadow take one step from its original state and then another. He closed his eyes again, to try to deepen his concentration, and then lost it all.

"No!" Mark's frustration erupted. He paced a few steps and gathered his composure.

"I'll try again," he told Marina.

"I'm sorry if you are disappointed that you couldn't perfect shadowing right away. I didn't want to affect your outcome by telling you that many have to practice for a long period of time before they can accomplish it."

"Some beings can do it immediately though?"

"Rarely, but yes.

"I like being the exception to the rule, so I'm going to try again," Mark said with determination.

He took a few deep breaths and consciously calmed himself. He entered a state of love and enjoyed the feeling of being next to her again. When he had successfully pictured his second foot leaving the soul, he slowed himself down and refocused on the love he felt for her. He consciously meditated on her and on sending his shadow to her. He realized that there were two points of view in his awareness. He concentrated harder. He felt a light breeze.

He could smell her. She was beside him. She looked at him and smiled. She was in a location that he didn't recognize. It was lush with greenery and glowing with golden sunshine. Could she see him? He called her name, and just as he did, he only saw Marina.

"Oh . . . oh . . . oh . . . holy shit!" he yelled. "I was there. I was there with her. She looked right at me, like she could see me. I was there!" Mark shouted. "I gotta go back, okay, I gotta go back—,"

"Mark, please listen to me. You have gone far enough for one day. You have proven to yourself that you can do it, but it will take practice. Don't exhaust yourself today. You saw her and she is fine, I assume?" Marina asked.

"She looked great, just how I remember her, the same age as when we met, which is about the age I am now. She looked happy and healthy." Mark was overjoyed.

"That is comforting to know, isn't it?" Marina asked. "So, take that thought home with you. Tell no one what has happened here today and come back tomorrow."

Mark resisted and tried to think of ways to convince Marina to let him keep trying.

"Mark, whatever you do, do not attempt to shadow yourself without a guide. I will have to teach your shadow how to find its way back to your soul. Once you project it out fully, it won't snap back like it did today. You have made fantastic progress. Be proud, get some rest, and come back tomorrow."

"Okay," Mark conceded. "I'll see you tomorrow."

CHAPTER THIRTY-TWO

Mark was very familiar with guilt. But he had never felt it as strongly as he did on the walk from Marina's campsite to Jonas's home. Mark knew that Jonas, Ellie, and Adam were trying to help him and he felt that he had betrayed them. Mark promised Marina that he wouldn't mention the experience, and he decided that keeping that promise was his best course of action for now.

Jonas's family was more animated than usual that night. They had used the fresh water to clean their home, do laundry, and take baths. The foursome felt spoiled and giddy. The children went to bed several hours later than usual. They were too excited to sleep. Jonas, who was usually conservative with the amount of time he allowed their candle to burn, didn't seem to notice as the wax inside the glass container transformed from solid to liquid.

After the children were asleep, Adam visited the family as promised. His physical youth matched his mood. He was thrilled about the progress that the Surface Dwellers were making toward independence.

The conversation eventually shifted to Mark's situation and Adam picked up where he had left off.

"It is true that the soul you knew as your son is here. Unfortunately, his Journey has been very challenging and he has forgotten that love is the strongest tool available for conversion. He has chosen to take matters into his own hands. He has been in this existence far longer than you have, Mark. His bitterness has deep roots. He has chosen tyranny, but you will be given the chance to help him remember who he really is. I know this because, as I told you, I have witnessed the Plan work trillions of times. It is no accident that you and he are here together. I urge you to believe that the chance to reconnect with him will reveal itself when the time is right. It will be very difficult to know that he is here and not begin looking for him," Adam said. "You must have faith in the Plan."

Mark puffed his cheeks and blew his entire lung capacity through his lips. "I trust you. You didn't need to tell me that he's here at all, and you did, so I believe that you're looking out for me."

"Don't forget that you have a mission on this Journey. Don't let yourself get so obsessed with looking back that you neglect your current Path," Adam told Mark.

"I don't know what that mission is yet, but I seem to be moving towards people who are more aware of the Journeys. I'm excited about what I'm learning from all of you." Mark looked at each face around the table. "Of course, I want to try to use the knowledge to end the torture of being separated from her. Especially if something evil is responsible for altering my Plan."

"Where did you get that idea? That evil was somehow responsible for diverting your Plan?" Jonas asked.

"What else could it be?" Mark asked. "I was aware that it had been decided that she and I would carry on together with the soul we created."

"There are no accidents, Mark. And there is no other force than love. But if you go looking for evil, even to try to fight it, you'll find evil, Mark." Ellie said softly.

"That is why shadowing is so dangerous. It isn't from The Spirit, which means it came from evil. He cannot protect you if you choose to use the resources of evil. Free will is a huge responsibility and it is given lovingly," Adam explained.

"The easy answer is hardly ever the right answer to solve any problem," Jonas told Mark.

"I know how tempting it will be to shadow yourself, Mark. I've seen your inner struggle in my mind and I feel your conflict in my heart. I ask that you remain in the light of love rather than giving into the temptation of the dark. None of us, not even The Spirit can reach into that world. If anything were to happen to your shadow, your soul would never be whole again. Enlightenment would be impossible for a soul in that condition. If something were to happen to your being while your shadow was outside of your soul, the same is true. It is a tremendous risk." Adam could see that his argument was not as strong as Mark's desire to be with her and that the risk was meaningless when compared to the slim chance that he could be successful in bringing her to his reality.

"Ask yourself this, Mark. Has Marina told you everything that we have about the dangers? Has she told you the source of her ability?" Adam asked.

Mark couldn't speak.

"It is best for us to let you think," Adam said as he rose from his chair. He let himself out of the house and Jonas and Ellie cuddled up with their kids in the corner.

Mark watched them take their children in their arms as they settled themselves.

It's easy to tell someone else what to do when you have your loved ones at your fingertips, he thought.

CHAPTER THIRTY-THREE

Packing eighty Trainees and Soldiers into the laundry room was difficult, but it was the safest place to meet.

Wentworth was surprised to see so many crewmembers at the meeting and he was nervous about their motives for being there. He cleared his throat and decided to act more confident than he felt.

"Every one of us could be court-martialed for conspiracy to mutiny," Wentworth said loudly as the chatter in the room died down. There were grunts and grumbles in reply.

"My name is Wentworth. You might have heard that I was left behind on the most recent supply drop to the Surface; but, as you can see, that is inaccurate. A lot of things on this ship are not as they appear and that's why we're here. I used to work in the General's office and the misinformation being circulated centers around me. I could be here to witness this meeting only to turn you all in tomorrow. My point is, we're going to have to trust each other." He tried to make eye contact with as many men as he could.

"Because, if I'm right, this Army is about to do some pretty nasty stuff to the Surface Dwellers that none of us agreed to be a party to when we signed up. I also have evidence that that an execution order was given for Lon Walker."

Some of the men at the meeting had not heard about Lon. They shook their heads and loud curses came from all corners of the room.

An Officer who had been sitting among the enlisted men stood up and walked toward Wentworth. He towered over the big trainee and his muscular frame threatened to burst the seams of his uniform. Wentworth swallowed hard. If the Officer was there to charge the men with treason, they were all as good as dead. And it looked like he could kill each of them by himself with his huge, bare hands.

"Wentworth, I think I'm the most senior crew member here. With your approval, I'll take the lead on this operation," he said. "You will need battalions of men on your side to oppose the General we formerly served and I think my experience will be of great help to you." Wentworth nodded his consent and the commanding officer turned to address the crew.

"For those of you who may not know me, I am Major Blake Kinsey. There are five other officers on board who will be with us. There are just over three hundred enlisted men and trainees who will be our opposition. We have our work cut out for us. Whoever wants to leave now may, with the understanding that you will not breathe a word of what you have heard here so far. If you stay, you're with us."

No one moved.

"Good choice, men. Let's get to work."

CHAPTER THIRTY-FOUR

Lon sprinted until his body demanded that he slow to a run, then a jog, then an unevenly paced walk. He was still making progress, but a freshly twisted ankle caused him to limp clumsily. He hoped that each uneven step would reveal the town on the horizon. When it didn't, he gathered all his energy for the next stride.

After seeing the Army's well-equipped Surface bunker, Lon guessed that they had tracking devices with night vision. He didn't know if they were watching him, but he figured that if they knew where he was, he'd already be dead. He hoped that he wasn't leading them to the town and to Mead.

Lon replayed the conversation he had with General Hilgers over and over again in his mind. Could his instinct to defend himself have been wrong? Maybe the Sergeant really was taking him to another barracks in an attempt to "*make him comfortable*" as the General had instructed him.

Lon put his hand in his pocket and wrapped his fingers around the weapon he now carried. To him, it was physical evidence that his gut feeling had been right. When the Sergeant was looking for Lon, he had been armed with the knife that he had held to Lon's throat. The fact that Lon took a gun off of him was proof that the General wanted Lon executed.

So why weren't they looking for him? Certainly they knew by now that he had severely beaten Humphries and had become the deserter they suspected him to be. The Army would not allow such acts to go unpunished. Lon decided that he should take cover and see if he could draw them out. He didn't want to be responsible for bringing the wrath of the Army onto the town. He lay down, buried himself with dirt, and waited.

CHAPTER THIRTY-FIVE

Mark hadn't slept all night; he was at war with himself. Seeing her yesterday, even for a moment, was the most wonderful experience he could have imagined. He knew that she had recognized him. She reacted to him. What must she think? Seeing him standing in front of her one second and watching him disappear the next must have made her crazy with worry. But Adam had been very convincing when he cautioned Mark against shadowing. The risk was—everything. Mark knew he couldn't let his current impatience jeopardize their eternity together in Enlightenment. But he couldn't stand the thought of her worrying about him after he popped in unexpectedly. He decided that he would shadow himself one more time to explain things to her.

When the family woke up, Mark already had breakfast waiting for them. He washed the dishes that they used, picked up the bedding and blankets, shook them out, and made sure that Ellie had no strenuous chores left to do after the family went about their daily routines.

"I'll be back before dinner, so don't lift a finger," Mark told her.

Ellie smiled. "I am going to go visit some who are far worse off than I am today. Would you like to come along?" she asked.

Mark sensed that she knew where he was headed.

"Not today, Ellie," he told her gently.

"Okay. I'll see you later this afternoon then." She made it easy for him.

Mark hadn't asked Marina what time he should come over, but he figured he would try his luck to see if she was around. He walked to her camp and found her sitting in a chair, sipping a glass of water.

"Mark! So happy to see you!" she greeted him.

"Thank you. I'm sorry to barge in, but you said I could come back today."

Her laugh put Mark at ease. "I have been expecting you," she told him. "Would you like a glass of water, or would you like to get started?"

"If you don't mind, I'm ready to go," Mark said eagerly.

"Let's go inside." Marina stood up and motioned towards the cloth she had hanging from a wire. Going behind the cloth was her definition of going inside.

"Do you remember how we started yesterday?" Marina asked.

"Yeah, I think I can get back there."

Mark focused his energy. It took several tries, but he eventually felt a gentle breeze and he knew that he had crossed the threshold.

She stood in front of him. Again she was in the middle of green vegetation, all by herself and, again, the sun shone brightly, making her dark hair glisten. Mark was speechless. After all this time, he was finally in the same place at the same time as she was.

"Hello," he whispered.

"Hey you." She smiled at him and her shoulders lifted along with the corners of her mouth.

"Do you know who I am?" he asked hopefully.

"Of course, silly."

"I'm sorry that I've been away from you, I've been trying to find you every minute--,"

"What do you mean?" She suddenly looked upset.

Mark didn't know what to say. He didn't want to alter her Journey by giving her information she shouldn't have yet.

"Never mind. I'm here now and that's all that matters."

"You're here, where you belong, and that is all that matters," she echoed.

"Are you okay?" Mark asked.

"Yes, everything is good."

"I love you so much," he whispered.

"I love you back." She smiled at him. "Are you okay? You seem . . . different somehow. Like you have something on your mind." She searched his eyes.

"I'm perfect," he answered. "Better than ever."

Mark became aware of his other perspective. Marina was directing him to see through the eyes of his vessel, but he didn't want to. His body was on another Tier and several existences away from where he wanted to be.

"Mark, it's time to return," Marina coaxed gently. "Change your perspective and come back."

Mark wanted to resist, but he was suddenly exhausted. "I have to go, but I'll be back." It was too easy to experience the complete joy of standing next to her—there was no way he could deny himself the pleasure of being with her.

"I'll be waiting," she assured him.

Mark experienced a softer landing into his being than what he had experienced the day before. It took a minute to recover from the dizziness that he felt and he gratefully accepted the glass of water that Marina offered him.

"I don't usually leave a student on another Tier for that long in the beginning," Marina told him. "But you seemed very much in control."

"A long time? I was only there for a few minutes."

"You were there all day, Mark. It's nearly time for the nightly meal."

Mark looked at the sky. It was already starting to get dark. He was confused, then panicked. "Shit! Ellie!" He remembered his promise to help Ellie get dinner ready. His feet started moving before his mind knew they were running. He turned and shouted over his shoulder, "Tomorrow?"

Marina laughed. "See you tomorrow."

Mark ran the short distance to Jonas's house. He burst through the door with an apology on the tip of his tongue, but it was quickly forgotten when he saw the family standing around the table. A man wearing charcoal gray pants was flat on his back on the small tabletop, his bare feet propped on a blanket-covered chair back.

"Walker?" Mark asked Jonas.

"Yes, but he is in terrible shape. Ellie's applying cool compresses and the children and I are fanning him to bring down his body temperature."

"When did he get here?" Mark asked.

"He showed up at the hospital about an hour ago. Ellie insisted that her assistants bring him here. He throws up everything we try to give him, but Ellie has some herbs under his tongue to try to settle his stomach. She thinks he has heat stroke."

Mark stepped over to the table and Sarah made room for him. "Walker, it's Wentworth. Can you hear me?"

Lon opened his eyes. "Mead," he whispered with a rasp through dry vocal chords. "Big . . . trouble," he said with much difficulty.

Mark absent-mindedly reached into the pocket of the pants that he inherited and felt the WA currency card that he still carried. Obviously Lon had seen the card, but that conversation could wait. So could whatever warning Lon wanted to convey. Mark thought that Walker probably wanted to tell him that switching ID tags with another trainee could get him into big trouble.

"Don't worry about trouble now, buddy. Just get better. You're safe here. Just rest."

Lon tried to speak again, but everyone shushed him. He didn't have the strength to argue, so he passed out.

* * * *

Jonas, Ellie, and Mark took turns nursing Lon through the night. During the moments when they were all awake at once, they speculated about him.

"He is not a very evolved soul, perhaps a Tier Two," Ellie guessed.

"How could he be here if he's a Tier Two?" Mark asked.

"Just because this realm is Tier Six for you doesn't mean it is the same for each Journeyer. We start together, but then each Plan requires different experiences at different times for each soul. That is why there are souls of different levels of awareness on every Tier," Jonas explained.

149

"We don't visit the Tiers in any particular order," Ellie told him. "We Journey to the circumstances that provide what we most need to learn."

Mark thought for a moment.

"So, Lon isn't aware of any Journey other than the one he is currently on?" Mark asked.

"I would guess that is true, based on his eyes," Ellie told him. "They are . . . " she searched for a kind way to say it, " . . . not very full."

Mark laughed. "He may not be evolved, but he was smart enough to figure out that I'm not Wentworth."

"You will have the opportunity to set the record straight soon enough," Jonas told Mark.

"If he lives," Ellie interjected.

Lon opened his eyes then as if to refute her fear. "Can you guys be quiet?" He whispered.

The three laughed with relief at his grumpy disposition.

"You got it, man. Get some sleep," Mark told him.

CHAPTER THIRTY-SIX

General Walthers couldn't contain his rage.

He plucked two hard-earned commendations from his office wall and, with a ferocious wail, whipped them, one by one, into the bulkhead. They made satisfying crashing and shattering sounds.

"Get me Wen--, I mean, Mead. Have him report to the Bridge on the double!" He shouted into the intercom that allowed him to talk to his assistant.

"Yes, Sir." The trainee from his office staff replied with an embarrassing tremor in his voice.

"I'd hate to be Mead right now. He must have really done it this time!" another trainee commented.

"Maybe he finally found evidence that Wentworth went AWOL and he wants to see what Mead knew about it—they were friends."

"C'mon, we worked with the guy every day. The WA was his life. He didn't defect and we all know that even if the General's paranoia is telling him otherwise." A third trainee finally said out loud what everyone had been thinking for the last eight days.

"There's no answer in Mead's quarters," the first trainee said in a whisper.

"Better report it fast. And don't remind him of your name in case he wants to shoot the messenger--," the trainee was interrupted by a new series of explosive crashing noises that came from the General's office. "And it's not my turn to clean up after him. I did it last time."

"Mead is not in his quarters," The assistant reported through the intercom.

"Then look someplace else and don't stop looking until you find him!" the General screamed loudly enough to render the intercom irrelevant.

The assistant grabbed his tablet and typed in the code for the squawk that commanded all crewmembers to report to their berths for inspection.

CHAPTER THIRTY-SEVEN

By mid-morning, Lon was able to sit up and eat a bowl of soaked grain. He washed it down with five glasses of water.

He told his story between bites while Jonas, Ellie, and Mark hung on every word.

Lon apologized to Mark profusely and repeatedly for revealing his identity to General Hilgers. Mark's only worry was that Wentworth would face a court-martial. He hoped that Went's exceptional record and his position in the General's office would warrant leniency.

"General Hilgers asked me if I knew anything about the construction of a filtration facility here and if I knew anything about whether the Dwellers had plans to rise up against the Army."

Jonas and Mark exchanged glances.

"Then he said I had been very helpful and ordered the Sergeant to make me comfortable. I thought it was weird that he was taking me from the security of the bunker and back to the turbulent Surface to '*make me comfortable*'."

"So, there is no way that you misjudged the order from General Hilgers or the Sergeant's actions? You're positive that they intended to kill you?" Mark asked.

"Why else would he need a gun?" Noncommissioned Officers don't get guns. You know that."

"Maybe they do on the Surface," Mark suggested.

"Doubtful. The World Army doesn't have enough weapons to equip all of its soldiers," Lon said matter-of-factly.

"I find it very troubling to know that there is an underground Army base within a couple day's walk of here." Jonas told Mark.

"I'm not convinced that the World Army soldiers are the bad guys," Mark shook his head. "What do we really know?"

"We know they didn't send the cavalry to rescue you two trainees; we know that they missed the weekly food drop; we know that they are randomly poisoning the food and water that they give to Surface Dwellers; we know that they watch us and regulate every aspect of our lives . . ." Jonas could have gone on, but Ellie quieted him by placing her hand over his.

"Mark, you will have to trust our experience. The World Army is not here to protect us as much as they are to dominate us," Ellie said. "We know that you and Lon don't have the same objectives, but you haven't been fully indoctrinated yet, have you?"

"I'm going to the Communication Center," Jonas told Ellie. "It sound like that base is closer to Gerard's town than ours. I should warn him. We also need to escalate the rate of our preparations. We don't have as much time to plan as we thought we did."

"Be careful." She kissed the back of his hand and he turned his palm to stroke her face.

After Jonas left, Mark finished the housework and Lon fell back to sleep.

"It's kind of crowded in here. I think I'm going to go for a walk and think things through," Mark told Ellie.

The Knower smiled at him and nodded her head.

CHAPTER THIRTY-EIGHT

Marina sat, patiently waiting, in the same chair where Mark had found her the day before. They wasted little time with idle chatter before sneaking behind the privacy of the hanging cloth to get started.

"I have to stay there longer today. I felt like I was only there for a few minutes yesterday. I barely got to say hello."

"Time is fickle. There is no measure of time and it doesn't translate from one Tier to the next. You get what you get," Marina explained.

"Okay, then let's start." Mark began the process.

He was able to shadow on the third try and found himself next to her again.

She was in the same location where he had visited her the first two times.

"I'm here," he said for both of their benefits.

"Good," she replied.

"I'm only complete when I'm here with you," he told her.

She smiled. "I'm worried about you," she said.

"I was worried about you too. That's why I'm here. I don't know how to do it yet, but I want to take you from here so that we can be together the way it was supposed to be," Mark explained.

156

"We are together."

"Right now, yes, but I mean forever. We were meant to Journey together the rest of the way. It was decided, and then --,"

She placed two fingers on his lips. "Shhhh, don't talk about that," She cooed.

Mark didn't know what to think. Was she afraid that they were being watched? Did she even know what he was talking about?

"Listen to me. I am coming to you from another Tier. I'm learning how to reconnect our souls here so that I can take you back with me," he explained.

"Stay here." She brightened at the thought. "It is so beautiful here. There is nothing to be afraid of, only light."

Mark had been so focused on her face that he had never really looked around. She was the only soul within sight. The green rolling hills went on until they touched a baby blue sky. Puffy white clouds drifted and danced overhead. The sunlight glowed and warmed the scene in harmony with the light breeze to maintain the perfect temperature.

"Are you alone here?" he asked.

"No." She smiled as if that was a silly question, "He is here. It's peaceful and I'm so happy here. Please stay with me. I'm not ready to leave."

Of all the reactions Mark imagined she might have when they saw each other again, this wasn't one he had anticipated.

"I'll see if I can. I'll see." He loved the sparkle in her eyes when he said something that made her happy.

"Please kiss me and never stop," she said.

"I'll try."

Mark was nervous about touching her. He hoped that it wouldn't break the spell.

He kept his eyes open so that he wouldn't miss one second with her. He leaned in close, caught a whiff of soap and orange blossoms, and gently placed his lips on hers. He felt her--he wasn't sure he would. Part of him worried that she was just an apparition. She responded to his kiss and pressed into him. He dared to raise his hand to her hair and found it to be as soft as he remembered. He wanted badly to keep the promise he made a few Journeys earlier, and few moments ago, to kiss her and never stop.

Over and over again, their lips found each other. And then Mark felt himself slipping away.

"I have to go," he explained. "I'll be back."

"I'll be waiting." She smiled.

The nausea that Mark had come to expect struck him as he returned to his being, but subsided quickly. Marina wasn't nearly as beautiful as he had first thought she was--not when compared to her.

"Can I stay there forever? On her Tier?" he blurted to Marina as soon as he recovered from the moment of blurry vision that accompanied the trips.

Marina smiled a sad smile. "A full soul cannot absorb a shadow because it is already complete. A shadow can absorb its perfect counterpart because there is room to do so," she told Mark.

"So, the only way for me to join her there is if she shadowed here to get me?" he clarified.

Marina nodded.

"Can I teach her? Or can you shadow with me to teach her next time?"

"It is against my beliefs to teach someone to shadow who has not come asking for the knowledge. It is against the traditions to seek out students. I only teach those who come with the knowledge of shadowing and seek my guidance."

"Shit!" Mark lost it again. "Why does this have to be so hard? Why are there so many stupid rules and hurdles and . . . shit?"

"You are shadowing very well. You are a very good student. I'm sure I will be able to teach you to connect with her so that you can bring her here. Your love is powerful and you will manifest her here," Marina assured him.

Mark spoke slowly and forcefully, "She doesn't want to come."

Marina nodded, "I see."

"She is there—alone from what I can tell, but she says *he* is there, whoever *he* is, and she says that it's beautiful and she's happy and she wants to stay. She asked me to stay with her." Mark put his hands to his head to stroke the smooth surface like he used to when he was upset, but found fuzz instead. He was surprised by the development and surprised by how out-of-touch he was with his person.

Marina nodded again. "I think I understand, Mark. Do you know if this is her first existence since you were separated?"

"I think it is, yeah."

"It sounds like she is in recovery. Sometimes, when a Journey is traumatic or the ending of the existence is traumatic, souls get damaged and aren't strong enough for a learning Journey. They need rehabilitation. It sounds as though that is the experience she needed and what she is doing right now."

"So, she isn't strong enough to leave there?"

"If she is still there, the indication is that she isn't ready."

"But, if losing me is what did that to her--damaged her--having me back would heal her," Mark reasoned.

Marina took a deep breath, "Not necessarily," she told him.

"I wish I had never seen her again. I wish I didn't know any of this." Mark left the area behind the privacy cloth and stomped out of Marina's camp.

"I'll be back tomorrow," he shouted loudly.

CHAPTER THIRTY-NINE

Jonas powered up the server and waited for the screen to come alive.

He checked for new communications, but there were none since the congratulations Gerard offered the last time they were in touch.

Jonas typed: *Must expedite preparations. Enemy camp located underground between us. Enemy is withholding supplies. Instinct is that conflict will happen sooner rather than later and not on our terms. Meet in three days. Please confirm.*

Jonas sent the message and powered the system down. It had used ten barrels of water to sustain enough energy to accomplish the task.

Jonas began to plan.

CHAPTER FORTY

Wentworth intercepted the message from his hiding place in the bilge of the ship.

His absence had been discovered when the General's assistant had called for all crewmembers to stand in front of their quarters. Major Kinsey had arranged several hiding places for him as the ship was being searched. None of them had been as bad as his new, smelly, hot, and humid home in the bilge.

Wentworth tried to guess what the General's reaction would be. He almost laughed at the thought of him turning purple with fury, but then he remembered that the General's fury could be very destructive.

CHAPTER FORTY-ONE

General Walthers quickly sent a message to General Hilgers:

Your location has been compromised. Walker is alive and has made contact with the Surface Dwellers. You have failed on your simple mission. I will clean up your mess.

Garrison Walthers had been waiting for this moment his whole career. But Mead was on the Surface and the action was coming to the Surface. The General had some decisions to make.

CHAPTER FORTY-TWO

Mark noticed that all of the foot traffic on the main path was heading in the same direction he was--to Jonas's house. When he arrived, he saw that the door was standing open and an overflow of men who couldn't make it inside were lined up all the way to the house that he had learned to count as "1" when he was using landmarks to find Jonas's home.

"What's going on?" Mark asked a guy his own age.

"We're signing up to defend the Dwellers. There's news that the Army has a base near here and we think they're gonna attack."

"Have you ever served in a militia or a military unit before?" Mark asked the kid.

He shook his head.

"Ever held a weapon?"

The kid shook his head again.

"I'm strong though. I've never lost a fight. If it comes down to fists, I'll take 'em all out," he bragged.

"Okay, buddy. Good luck." Mark feigned belief and patted him on the back. With a little effort, Mark worked his way through the men and into the packed house where Lon and Jonas sat at the kitchen table. Lon still looked terrible, but he was fueled by a sense of purpose.

"Sign your name here and come back after the sun sets. We start training tonight," Lon told a boy who couldn't have been much older than ten.

"Did I miss something?" Mark approached the table where Jonas and Lon were sitting.

"That base has been operating for a long time, judging by what Lon told us about it. They have had far more time to prepare than we have, so I decided that there's no time like the present to start training our soldiers," Jonas replied.

"Soldiers? That last kid was barely out of diapers." Mark exaggerated to make his point. "Jonas, this can't be the only way. Taking up arms can't be the only way. You must *know* a way to change the situation without killing." Mark referred to Jonas' enlightened soul without saying as much in front of Lon.

"I know this much, Mark; we do have the most powerful force on our side, but we will have to be alive to use it. These people will need to know how to defend themselves against an attack. Our declaration of independence was not likely to have been met with acceptance; but, if we are attacked, that is completely different. We must be as prepared as we can possibly be to defend our loved ones."

The line of men from the town moved quickly. The last man signed up and closed the door to the house as he was leaving.

Jonas counted the names. "Our militia is seventy-four men strong."

Mark didn't want to be a defeatist, but he hoped to be the voice of reason. "With seventy-four guys to stand between the town and the blaster, we're nothing more than a smudge on their fly swatter."

"That's why we can't let the shuttle land. The blaster can't fire if it's airborne," Lon reminded him.

"Can you train these men to give them a tactical advantage if the Army attacks?" Jonas asked Lon.

"With Mark's help, yeah."

Jonas and Lon both looked at Mark. "I'll follow Walker's lead. I'm kind of obligated since he saved my life and all," Mark joked.

He was glad that Lon was the one in charge of the effort. An effective leader should have a shred of hope that more than a handful could survive. Lon seemed to think they had a fighting chance, but Mark didn't agree.

He also worried that Jonas was overreacting. The base had obviously been out there for a very long time; it was well established. Whatever the mission of the Surface Unit was, Mark didn't believe that it was a command post for launching attacks against the Dwellers. Maybe the function of the Unit was to observe the Surface Dwellers and gather intelligence. To Mark, that theory explained the Top Secret nature of the Surface Base. If Mark's guess was right, Jonas's reaction might be more dangerous than the base itself.

CHAPTER FORTY-THREE

Kinsey walked down the long line of huge clothes dryers in the laundry. As he passed each one, he placed his flat palm on the door. When he found the one that was cool to the touch, he popped it open.

Wentworth hung his long legs over the side of the appliance and hopped out of the front-loading door. "It's a good thing that I'm not claustrophobic," he said.

"I'm doing the best I can to keep you ahead of the search team, but the reward money is making bounty hunters out of half the crew."

"I'm not complaining. You're in charge of the search, so I know I'm safe. Just keep in mind that I'm not a contortionist," Wentworth said. He twisted his torso from side to side to get the kinks out. "I intercepted messages from the Surface, Walthers, and Hilgers." Wentworth handed his tablet to Kinsey so he could read the communications himself.

"I'll tell the rest of the Brothers," Kinsey said.

"Brothers?"

"Oh, right. While you were in the dryer our movement was given a name. You are an associate of the mutinous force that has been branded *The Brothers of the Rebellion.*"

"I hope the guys spent some time thinking about strategy. It's nice that we know what to print on the T-shirts, but naming the group wasn't my top priority."

"It's important for the troops to belong to a movement. Since they named it we've grown to one hundred and twenty-five members. We have over 25% of the total crew now," Kinsey said.

"Good. Very good." Wentworth nodded his approval. "Anything new on the General's daily agenda—any training exercises or formal notices?"

"Nothing, but we're watching. We'll be ready," Kinsey assured Wentworth.

"Where am I going next?"

"I have to let the search team cross the laundry off their list—I'm afraid your next hiding place won't smell as fresh as this one did."

Wentworth took the tablet back from the Major. "Lead the way."

CHAPTER FORTY-FOUR

Lon was in his glory. He paced back and forth in front of the men who were lined up in seven and a half rows of ten across. Lon adopted the same speech pattern and impossible volume as the Majors who taught combat training on the battleairship. He extended every centimeter of his five-foot-ten inch frame and bellowed at the men, "Our mission is to fend off an attack from a more advanced, more capable, and better trained adversary. We are outnumbered, out-skilled, out-gunned, and out-everythinged that you can imagine. We don't have a chance."

Lon stopped pacing and faced his raggedy bunch of troops, "That's what *they* think. But they are wrong. And underestimating your enemy is tactical suicide. I guarantee you that the World Army believes that you are stupid, weak, and unprepared. I promise you that they are not increasing their training drills in anticipation of squashing the Surface Dwellers. I assure you that, if they are deployed to come here to eradicate us, that they will consider the mission a one-blast quickie and they will anticipate declaring a victory before breakfast."

Mark stood behind Lon and listened to his speech. He assessed the troops and could tell that Lon's speech had captured the full attention of the unimpressive bunch, from the very young recruits to the terribly old ones.

"We have the advantage of knowing exactly what they are capable of, what their training tells them to do, and how they will be armed. We know . . . *exactly*. They have no idea that we have assembled, that we began training tonight, or that we know how to exploit their weaknesses."

The men looked at each other and mumbled—all of a sudden each man knew several ways in which the Army was vulnerable.

"At attention!" Lon shouted. The misfit militia quieted and stood tall again. Lon stood looming in front of them, his average build seemed to swell with the confidence he exuded.

"When we combine our talents, our knowledge, and our expertise, we will become a formidable foe for our enemy. If they are unwise enough to attack us on our own land, we will use our resources in ways they never expected to defeat them."

A hand shot up in the crowd and Lon acknowledged the young man who wished to speak.

"I have four shot guns and eight boxes of ammunition," he said softly. "You can have 'em."

The men turned to look at youngster with astonishment.

"I have a hand gun," someone else called out from the back.

"Don't know if it still shoots, but I got one too."

The men were surprised and excited to hear that there were weapons in their town. They reacted to the news with shouts of surprise and elation.

Mark pitied the militia's naïve enthusiasm about their armaments—six weapons were not going to change the momentum of the fight.

"At attention, men!" Lon yelled again. The energized troops regained their composure.

"Men, we will make sure that their crafts will not have the opportunity to land here and discharge a blaster. If our enemy attacks, we will defeat them. Our triumph starts tonight."

Lon walked over to stand next to Mark. "Let's see what you're good at," he challenged the men. "We can't afford to expend rounds, but we can test your aim, your hand-to-hand combat skills, and your basic levels of fitness. Half of you will come with me, half will go with Mead and we'll find out where you will be most useful to this militia," Lon concluded.

Mark shook his hand when the speech was over. "Well done. I'm impressed."

"We are going to be the target of a full-scale land and air attack," Lon said under his breath. "We're as good as dead."

"Roger that," Mark agreed.

CHAPTER FORTY-FIVE

Marina sat calmly in her chair as Mark paced back and forth.

"So, you're running. I guess I can't blame you. This place is going to be a war zone." Mark stopped pacing and faced Marina.

"This isn't my fight. I don't feel like I'm running. I'm keeping myself safe," Marina told him. "If you are truly concerned for your mate's safety, maybe you should wait to bring her here until after the conflict."

"You're the only one I know who can help me, Marina. I waited three lifetimes to be with her and I'm not taking the chance of losing touch with her again. I'll worry about keeping her safe. All you have to do is help me get her here."

Mark's anguish showed on his face and could be heard in his voice. "Please see this through. Please don't leave until I have her back. If you tell me exactly how to connect with her, I will bring her back with me today," he begged.

"If she is resistant to coming back, you won't be able to bring her here against her will. She will have to be fully and completely dedicated to attaching to you," Marina warned.

"She'll listen to me. How do I do it?"

"It's simple. You hug her and hold her to you. With willing souls, they merge themselves. You will, essentially, absorb her," Marina told him.

"When I shadow, I feel like I'm getting pulled back into my being," Mark told her. "Yesterday, I felt like I faded out of there."

"That is my doing," Marina admitted. "I watch your being. I don't want you to risk overexertion. If you don't have the energy to come back, your shadow will get stuck."

"Let me stay there until I have her, okay? Don't pull me." Mark instructed her.

"I have never lost anyone, Mark. I don't want you to be my first."

"If I only have one shot at this, you have to give me time. I'm not exactly an expert. I need to know that you aren't going to pull me back until I've connected with her."

"I will not allow you to be in jeopardy. Perhaps you should look for a more careless guide." Marina stood up from her chair as if she was going to walk away.

Mark reached out and gently took her arm. "Wait . . . wait, okay? Listen, I don't want another guide. I'm thankful for your protectiveness. Please, just promise to give me every possible second there, okay?"

Marina faced Mark and her eyes were filled with compassion. "I will leave you with her as long as I am able to do so," Marina promised.

"Thank you. I'll see you soon." Mark smiled and winked at Marina before he focused his attention on transporting his shadow.

On the first try, Mark found himself on the Fourth Tier. He looked around for her, but saw nothing other than the rich landscape. He focused his love for her and waited for the manifestation of the golden glow to show him where she was, but it didn't come.

He started to panic, but fought to control his mind. If he slipped from a loving state, he would snap back into his being and he needed to stay here. If she needed him, he had to be here for her.

He focused on loving the ability to remain in her realm and he felt that there was power in that emotion. Mark felt fully present on Tier Four and refocused on finding her.

"Hello?" He called out. "I'm back. Just like I said I would be."

There was no reply.

"You said you would be waiting," he called as he walked through the soft grass. The wind blew gently and the sun warmed him.

He fought another panic-inducing thought. What if she had left the Tier? What if she was in the Transition Tier? What if she was being sent somewhere else?

Mark remembered that Marina had instructed him to set his course for *whom* and not *where*. So, even if she was somewhere else, he should have been able to go to her.

"Hello?" he called again. "It's me. It's Mark. Your soul mate, the love of your life, the father of your son!" He was feeling desperate and had to willfully create the love that held him there.

175

He felt himself slipping back. "No!" he shouted in case Marina could hear him. "Please, no!"

But seconds later, he was standing in front of Marina.

Before he could gather himself enough to speak, Marina began to apologize.

"I know I said I would leave you there as long as possible, but you were in such a state of distress, I feared for your soul, Mark--,"

"She wasn't there!" Mark screamed. Fear consumed him, tears formed in his eyes and his voice broke when he spoke. "What does that mean?"

"I--," Marina shook her head. "I don't know."

Mark grabbed her by the shoulders, "What do you mean you don't know? Has this ever happened before?"

"Not to me."

"Have you ever heard of this happening to anyone else?" Mark questioned her.

"I think I heard my father talking about it, but I was so young, I don't remember any of the details," Marina put her face in her hands and Mark sat her down in her chair.

"Is she okay? If she moved from that Tier, would I have gone to her new Tier, or is she in limbo somewhere? Since The Spirit doesn't approve of shadowing, could she be in the Transition Tier? I wouldn't be allowed to go there, so would my shadow go to where she was last?" Mark talked to the back of Marina's hands.

"I don't know, Mark. I'm so sorry, but I just don't know."

"Well, I gotta go back and look some more, then. Maybe she was there and I just landed in a different location. Maybe I didn't spend enough time looking for her."

"Mark, you were there all day. The sun went down hours ago," Marina pointed out the obvious.

Mark heard the militia marching past the front of Marina's camp with Lon calling out the cadence.

"Shit!" Mark was torn between his need to get back to Tier Four and his commitment to Jonas's doomed militia.

"Don't you dare leave until you figure this out," Mark commanded Marina. "Talk to whoever you have to talk to, do whatever you have to do. I'll be back later tonight and I want answers," Mark said forcefully.

"I'll do my best," Marina assured him.

CHAPTER FORTY-SIX

What the militia lacked in experience, they made up for in dedication. The men ranged in age from nine to sixty-eight. There was an argument between Dean and another man about who was the most senior member of the militia. They both claimed the privilege that they assumed came with the title, but neither could remember their exact age, so the verbal confrontation was short lived and ended in laughter.

Lon had led the group on a three-mile run/jog/walk and had demonstrated basic conditioning exercises by the time Mark showed up.

"I though you went A.W.O.L.," Lon remarked when he joined the group.

"Sorry," Mark muttered, regretting his choice to be with the militia rather than staying at Marina's.

"We're going to take target practice with these metal sling shots that Dean made," Lon informed Mark. "You wanna take a group over by that target and show them how to use the sights?"

"Sling shots," Mark muttered to himself. He knew that this was a waste of his precious time.

"Sent a two pound rock about ten yards," Dean bragged.

"That'll come in handy," Mark said approvingly, but he couldn't imagine the scenario that would make his statement true.

"It's more for the sake of getting used to lining up sights." Lon read Mark's mind.

"Yeah, I get it. It's a good idea," Mark said, trying to sound enthusiastic.

He didn't realize how foreign the concept of target practice would be to people who spent most of their time busying themselves with survival. There was nothing to hunt on the Surface, so shooting was a skill that had never been necessary to perfect. Mark taught the men how to line up the shot using the sight and how to deliver the rock to the target where they were aiming.

Most were still tired from running and doing calisthenics and they barely had the strength to draw the tension band, let alone do it deliberately enough to aim.

"How are the slingshots working?" Dean asked eagerly while he was waiting for his turn.

"They're well built, old man. Heavy, but well-balanced." Mark patted his friend on the back. "Where did you find the rubber?"

"Traded for it. Word traveled to a town nearby that we have water. You wouldn't believe what people bring me for clean water. If I had the filtration system, I could have traded for all the parts to build it ten years ago." Dean laughed.

"Funny how that works. Can't get enough of something when you need it, but are drowning it in when you don't." Mark shook his head.

"How's it going with Marina?" Dean asked in a whisper.

"Good until today. I've shadowed successfully three times now, but today she wasn't there. Or I couldn't find her when I got there," Mark corrected himself. "You ever experience anything like that?"

"No, man. I have work to do when I shadow, I'm not just a tourist."

"Marina is going to ask around to see if anyone knows what it means. Maybe when I go back later tonight, I'll find her again. Maybe I went to the wrong place."

Dean shook his head. "Or, whatever evil kept you apart before found out you were getting back together and separated you again."

Mark was furious at the casual way Dean brought up such a horrible and unlikely possibility.

"We think differently about that, Dean. We already had this debate," Mark said firmly turning his attention to the next man in line.

"No one ever wants to hear the truth," Dean muttered as he walked away.

Mark worked with every man in his line until they were hitting the target at least fifty-one percent of the time. They would refine their skill the following night.

To end the training session, Lon gave a lecture about what to expect during an air attack and how they would best combat it. About the time the sun was rising, the training session was over.

CHAPTER FORTY-SEVEN

Major Kinsey stood in front of the assembled and burgeoning Brothers of the Rebellion. They reported information from the various areas of the battleairship where they worked. Overall, the only noticeable difference in the daily routine on the ship was the search for Wentworth who, for the moment, was safely stuffed in Kinsey's locker.

"So what's our plan if we're given orders to attack the Surface?" A newcomer asked Kinsey.

"We have Brothers in every department of the battleairship--the laundry, the engine room; everywhere from the navigation station to the Bridge. We even have three of the ten who work inside the General's office on our side and they're keeping their eyes open." Kinsey paused for effect. "And we have the Quartermaster." Kinsey was satisfied with the Brothers' surprised reaction.

"If the command to attack is given, it will be through the Quartermaster as a General Quarters call to battle stations, as you know. We will have the tip because our Brother will be sounding the whistle. The first step is to overthrow the General's authority. That will have to be done forcefully, and will probably take place on the Bridge, since that's where the order would be handed down from. We are trying to feel out the other trainees on the Bridge to see if more of them would be sympathetic to our cause. The more guys we have on our team up there, the better.

Once we take command of the Bridge, the rest will be easy. We have men who can stall and give us time along every phase of the procedural checklist for launching an attack. Before the soldiers loyal to the General realize that the power has changed hands, we should have access to all launch codes and have the blaster disabled. The power lies with those who control the weapons. I feel confident that very few GIs will try to be heroes and retain control of the ship. The General has a few loyal guys; but, for the most part, this Army has a very individual mentality." Kinsey finally said out loud what he had been thinking for years. "It's hard to inspire loyalty to a cause when there is no real threat from an enemy."

"So, for now, we go about our business as usual and wait for the signal?" a soldier asked.

"The signal will be the Quartermaster's whistle for General Quarters. When you hear it, secure your area. If that means disabling soldiers who resist, you have my authorization to do so," Kinsey said.

"Be careful, Major, you're starting to sound a lot like the General," the soldier warned.

CHAPTER FORTY-EIGHT

Mark hadn't slept, but, tired as he was, he didn't consider resting. As soon as the militia disbanded and went about their daily routine, he started walking back to Marina's.

Adam had to call his name three times to get his attention. Mark popped out of his haze and looked around to see who had been yelling to him.

"I've been sprinting after you and still couldn't keep up," Adam told him. "Is everything all right?"

"Yeah, everything is fine. I'm just in a hurry." Mark tried to excuse himself.

Adam motioned for Mark to bend down so that he could whisper to him. "We never got another chance to talk after we discussed shadowing." Anyone looking on would have thought that Adam was asking for help or advice from his elder.

"I am worried that the temptation may have been too much for you." Adam tried to make it easy for Mark to confess. "I would understand, of course, if you hadn't been able to resist."

Mark thought about telling him everything that he already seemed to know. Adam might even have some insight into where she might be or what happened the last time Mark sent his shadow to her.

Then he remembered Marina's demand that he not tell anyone about what they were doing. Right now, Marina was the only tangible link to his love and he couldn't risk alienating her.

"Thank you, Adam, from the bottom of my heart, for your concern. I am trying to do what is right," Mark told him. *I'm trying to make something right, anyway,* he thought.

"My brother, I am always here for you if you should have any questions or if you just need someone to talk to. It seems that we are facing uncertain times and that war may be coming to us. Many of us will face personal struggles and we can overcome adversity together if we choose the right Path."

"Thank you," Mark said again. He forced a smile and resumed walking in the direction of Marina's house.

When he got there, he could see that she hadn't slept all night either.

"I think it is best that we try again to find her on Tier Four. I haven't been able to come up with an explanation as to why she wasn't there last night. Before we take action on the assumption that she has departed, we had better be sure." Marina hadn't even waited for Mark to say hello.

"Agreed," Mark said as he parted the cloth door that would give them some privacy.

Mark deliberately loved her, not in the abstract way that he was capable of when he was on Tier Three, but in a measurable, concrete manner. The force of love built rapidly and he was propelled to Tier Four.

When Mark got there, she was not standing in front of him as she had been the first few times. He tried calling for her again, but there was no answer. Mark tried walking around the realm, but he found that the landscape seemed to roll under his feet like a hamster wheel. He was convinced that she was not there.

Thinking that there was no time to waste, Mark began to will his shadow back to his soul, but just as he began to refocus his perspective, something changed. He made himself fully present in the moment and watched for more movement.

"Hello?" Mark called out. "I feel you there. Come out where I can see you."

When the figure began to take shape in front of him, Mark started to cry.

"Marcus!" Mark screamed out, his voice filled emotion.

The boy ran to his father, "Daddy!"

Marcus jumped into his father's arms for the first time in two existences.

"Marcus, I have been looking for you!" Mark's tears fell freely down his face as he intermittently looked into his son's eyes and hugged him tightly.

"Daddy," Marcus cooed.

"Son, have you seen your mother here? I just found a way to reach her and then I lost her again," Mark explained to the little boy.

"You're good at losing people, aren't you Dad?" The little boy's voice took on an adult quality.

Mark reacted as if he had been punched. He held the boy at arm's length. This was the little boy he knew as Marcus, but there was more to him now. Mark gently lowered him to the landscape and kneeled down in front of him so that they were eye to eye.

"You can't keep anyone safe, can you? I tried to tell you about the shadows that came to my room at night, but you didn't listen. You were too focused on her to care that I was in danger, I guess." Marcus's voice was still his, but far more mature; deeper than Mark remembered.

"What are you talking about, son? What shadows?" The gentle breeze and perfect temperature had remained constant in the beautiful setting, but Mark shuddered from a terrible chill.

"The shadows came into my room almost every night. They watched me, but they couldn't touch me. It was horrifying!"

"I thought you were having nightmares." Mark remembered the phase that his son was talking about.

"I told you it was real!"

Mark's heart went out to his son. "I'm so sorry that you still remember. It must have been very upsetting for you if it still bothers you so much. I'm very sorry."

"Are you sorry that you let the shadow get me that night on the boat? Or are you only sorry that they took her away from you?"

Mark suddenly felt overwhelming fear. He fought to maintain a state of love.

"I don't know what you mean." Mark swallowed hard to keep his composure and bits of memories flashed into his consciousness.

"The shadows caused the storm. When the waves got violent enough and the boat sank, they pulled us, well, me, away from you. You hung onto her with all your strength. You fought for her, but you let me go!" The boy's accusation was filled with hatred. Mark tried to place his hands on Marcus' shoulders, but the small boy shrugged him off.

"I didn't know—I don't remember . . . " Mark struggled to replay the memory of that night as he had struggled to do for the last two Journeys.

"The shadows finally came for me, they could finally touch me and you let them have me!" The boy screamed through his tears. His nose ran, his face turned bright red, and spit flew from his mouth when he yelled.

"I would never let anything take you away from me. I didn't see the shadows. I never saw a shadow," Mark tried to convince Marcus. "The storm surprised us all. The weather had been clear that night. It was a perfect night for a sunset sail. I took every precaution when taking you out in the boat, but the weather came up from nowhere and when the boat failed, I held you both--," Mark stopped talking and started crying again. "That's all I can remember," Mark told Marcus. "I have never been able to go past that point, where I'm struggling with all my physical strength, all my love, to hang on to you."

"You hung on to her. You let me go, and then you fought for her. But you lost us both didn't you, Dad?"

"We were supposed to go to the Transition Tier together and then onto the next Journey together. I knew that. It had been decided," Mark told Marcus.

"We couldn't get there from the darkness. There is no Path that leads there from the darkness!"

Mark tried to pull the boy close to him, but Marcus struggled out of his grasp.

"While you Journeyed through your next Tier, we were trapped in darkness, terrified as the shadows moved among us. She kept telling me that you would come for us. She never gave up hope, but I knew that you were too weak to confront them. You lived in a world where there were only possibilities for good. Just because you don't believe in evil doesn't mean it doesn't exist."

"I looked for you. As soon as I had reached an age where I could access my memories, I started looking and never stopped. And I asked to be with you again in the Transition Tier, but the Plan had changed, so I tried to increase my faith--,"

Marcus went from crying to laughing hysterically. "Well, you're gonna need that faith, Dad." Marcus mocked. "We'll see how that helps you out now."

"How did you get out of the darkness, Marcus?"

"I made a deal. That's the only way out. After about eighty years in the darkness, you realize that your Daddy isn't going to save you and that The Spirit doesn't want to get His hands dirty. You watch your beloved mother lose control of her mind a little more every day and you do whatever it takes. I had already lost myself, so what did it matter?" Marcus shrugged nonchalantly.

"What did you do?"

"I think you know what I did. I took a little detour from the Journeys, stopped jumping through The Spirit's hoops. You're either playing for one team or another," Marcus told his father.

"He will forgive you. You can come back to Him, son. I'll help you," Mark pleaded.

"Little late, Dad. And aren't you forgetting about her? Where is your precious wife?" Marcus looked around the scene.

"She was happy here. She was rehabilitating her soul here. This was the Journey she needed to take before she continued on her Path," Mark told his son.

"I saved her from the darkness. *I* did. Not you. I gave up everything so that she could be free again. You moved on without us as if we never existed. I had convinced myself that you deleted us, but knowing that you remembered us and didn't do anything—you just went on with your own Journeys--you're far more horrible than I thought you were."

189

Mark grabbed Marcus's face and forced him to look into his eyes. "That is not true. I did everything in my power. I am here as a shadow right now, against the laws, to try to connect again." Mark realized something. "I was told that you were on my Tier. I was coming here to get her and bring her to the Tier where you and I are . . ." Mark trailed off. "You're shadowing right now." The shock of the knowledge made his hands falls from Marcus' face.

"You're new to this aren't you? Yes, I'm shadowing. In the vessel that you remember. I gave this up." Marcus swooped his hands from head to toe. "I'm a far more intimidating being now. Right when I had you where I could keep an eye on you and execute my plan to show you exactly how much pain Mom and I had been through because of your betrayal, you slipped away."

"What are you doing here?" Mark asked him. "What have you done with her?"

"Protecting her from you!" Marcus yelled. "When she told me that you had been here . . ." Marcus couldn't find the words to express his anger.

Mark remembered that she mentioned she wasn't alone on this Tier. Marcus had been shadowing in to check on her.

"We have the same goal, Marcus. You and I have the exact same goal. We both want for all of us to be together as a family, the way it was meant to be."

"You might as well go back to your pitiful being, Daddy." Marcus mocked him.

"Where is she?" Mark asked evenly, fighting to control his panic.

"She is all you care about. She's all you ever cared about." Marcus shook his head. "We'll see who wins this battle, Dad. Good luck," he said, then he faded away.

"No!" Mark felt himself being pulled back. He was aware of the shift in is consciousness and then Marina and Adam were standing in front of him. Mark began to sob.

CHAPTER FORTY-NINE

Sarah and John were still making their daily contributions to the town. Jonas, Ellie, Adam, and Mark sat around the family's kitchen table. Adam told the Knowers about Mark's encounter on Tier Four and, when he finished, silence hung over them for several minutes.

Finally, Jonas spoke. "It's useless to look back when there is so much to face ahead. Tell us, Adam, what should we do now?"

"I can only see that Marcus is on this Tier. I can't see where," Adam told them.

"Marina thinks that he was able to transport his mother from Tier Four since part of her lives in him," Mark said.

"The parent and child connection is the strongest soul connection," Ellie confirmed.

"So he has her?" Mark asked.

"Yes, but it doesn't seem likely that he would hurt her. In his immature way, he is trying to protect her," Ellie assured Mark.

"She's probably right here on this Tier, if that comforts you. That's why you couldn't shadow to her. You can't send a shadow to the Tier you occupy," Adam explained.

"I got the feeling that she was very fragile. If the Plan was for her to stay on Tier Four until she was ready to leave, it might be dangerous for her to be here," Mark said.

"That's true. Tier Four is where she is meant to be until The Spirit knows she is ready to move onward," Adam agreed.

"Is there anything we can do?" Mark asked.

"We increase our faith, we ask for guidance, and we wait," Adam told him.

"There's always the possible conflict with the World Army to take our minds off of my problems," Mark tried to joke.

"We will do what we can," Ellie said matter-of-factly.

"I'm so sorry." Mark met the eyes of each person at the table. Love reflected back at him.

"We're sorry for the pain you feel, Mark." Jonas spoke for everyone.

Lon swung the door open and burst into the house, "Jonas, I have a message from the Communications Center. Gerard will be here tomorrow and he is bringing another hundred militia members to train!"

"You asked what was next . . ." Adam smiled at Mark who was too exhausted to return the gesture.

CHAPTER FIFTY

He had become an expert at shadowing and his vessel could function very well while a large part of him was outside of it. When he changed his perspective, he found himself sitting at his desk across from one of his office staff drones. The young soldier was reporting on the search for Wentworth and was using a million words to avoid saying that the trainee had not been found.

Seconds earlier on Tier Four, Garrison Walthers had faced his most hated adversary. He had waited nearly three full lifetimes for the confrontation and it had been satisfying—the shock on Mead's face had been priceless, but his insolence had been infuriating. The emotions brought up by that encounter made it difficult to play the role of an Army General engrossed in an uneventful report.

The General interrupted his office staffer mid sentence. "Who sympathizes with the filthy Dwellers?"

"Sir?" The soldier blinked. The General had been sitting perfectly still and had seemed to be listening attentively for the last ten minutes. Now the soldier wondered if he had been heard at all—he hadn't been talking about sympathizers.

"We haven't docked or landed since this trainee went missing and he didn't go for a swim in the wild blue yonder. If we can't find him, that means someone is hiding him. Perhaps he has a contingent of soldiers working for him and against me. Maybe half my crew is deceitful." General Walthers tilted his head to one side and considered his statements with an odd smile on his face.

"Dimissed," he barked at the soldier.

"Sir, yes Sir." The soldier nearly ran from the General's office.

Alone now, General Walthers put his feet up on his desk, stacking his size thirteen combat boots one on top of the other, and leaned back in his chair.

"That's okay," he said speaking out loud to the only person he trusted. "I don't give a shit if half the crew is untrustworthy. Once I expose the filtration facility on the Surface, I'll have justification for an attack. I'll obliterate the rodents on the Surface and send dear old Dad off to the next Tier at the same time. Useless General Hilgers can find out about the attack on the Surface at the same time the Dwellers do. If he responds with humility and respect, maybe I will allow him and his regimen to live. Maybe I will even invite him to attend the ceremony when the Army promotes me to Supreme General."

The General closed his eyes and relished the moment of satisfaction that accompanied his resolve. Suddenly startled, he jumped to his feet and looked around the room wildly. Seeing nothing out of order, he locked his desk, barged through the outer office, and left the bridge.

CHAPTER FIFTY-ONE

Mark walked to the outside of the town to be alone with his emotions. His hair had grown long enough to be messy and his beard was scruffy. He felt dirty, ashamed, and tired beyond belief. He didn't search for cover or try to bury himself in the earth as he knew some wanderers did. He simply walked until he couldn't anymore and lay down where he stopped. He was flat on his back and asleep within seconds of leaving his feet.

The warmth of the supposed sun comforted him and relaxed his bones. He was peaceful in spite of his current circumstances.

As he often did, Mark dreamed of Tier Three. He dreamed of happy times with his wife and son. He heard their laughter and felt their hugs. In the dream he was aware of feeling good in his skin, not sticky and gritty as he had become used to lately. Mark slept soundly, entertained by the visions that played in his mind.

Then she was beside him. He didn't open his eyes or move, and he didn't know if he was asleep or awake. She asked him to listen to her and to believe her. She told him that they were coming for him. They were coming by air. The battleairship was deploying a shuttlecraft to attack him. His eyes sprung open after her final words, "Be ready."

Mark was on his feet in an instant. He didn't know—didn't care—if it had been a dream or a premonition. When he heard something true, it resonated in him.

Without another thought, he began sprinting back to town to spread the word—they were coming.

CHAPTER FIFTY-TWO

Wentworth was suspicious of the lack of messages being transmitted aboard the ship. His tablet had only pinged ten times in four hours, most of which were messages that were automatically generated. He sensed that something had changed, but he couldn't exactly claim to have his finger on the pulse of the battleairship. He had been traveling in laundry baskets, between crewmembers' quarters, the locker room, the engine room, the galley, the dry storage areas, and wherever else the Brothers of the Rebellion had arranged to hide and guard him. Wentworth felt like a hot potato.

He gave the prearranged signal to the trainee guarding his hiding spot. The area was safe and the guard responded, "Come on out and stretch if you need to."

Wentworth lifted the top of the lazaret. He had been lying down inside of a long seating bench in the media center. Wentworth felt like he was crawling out of a coffin and shivered at the thought. He recognized his guardian as Billy Thomas, a trainee from the class one year junior to his own.

"Can you reach Major Kinsey for me?" He asked Thomas.

"I don't know where he is, but I'll get the word out." He pointed at Wentworth's tablet. "You have new intel?"

"It's too quiet, actually. I haven't gotten anything new and that's what worries me."

"Like radio silence?" Thomas asked innocently.

"Exactly like radio silence," Wentworth confirmed. "What's it like in the passageway?" He pointed to the closed door.

Thomas poked his head out. "Typical Sunday." He described the one day each week that most crewmembers only left their rooms for meals.

"Give me your hat and your glasses," Wentworth commanded. Even though the trainees were the same rank, the younger one deferred to the crusader who had dared to start the pending mutiny.

"Where am I most likely to find Kinsey?" He asked.

"My best guess would be the Mess," the trainee answered.

Wentworth went into the passageway and headed for the Mess. He passed a few soldiers and an Officer, but walked with purposeful confidence so that he didn't draw attention.

When he finally got to the crewmember's dining room, he saw Kinsey right away. He was sitting across from the General. The General never took his meals in the Mess.

Wentworth's instinct was to turn and run, but he decided that type of behavior was consistent with what the *old* Wentworth would do. The Wentworth/Mead hybrid was determined to do what had to be done in spite of his fears.

He went through the food line without saying a word to anyone. He loaded his plate—as hard as the Brothers worked to sneak him food, he hadn't been getting enough to eat. He took his tray and sat down two seats away from the General, facing the same direction that he was.

Wentworth's heart was beating fast. He didn't want to imagine what would happen to him if he were discovered. He knew that the General had made it a priority to locate him, and the fact that he was still in hiding was an embarrassment and a frustration.

"The Dwellers wish they were eating like this today," The General said loudly. "Why are we treated to the fine lives that we have? Because of our dedication to the World Army, that's why. We are loyal soldiers and the Army rewards us for our bravery and our willingness to take action. Those Dwellers don't have the intellect, ambition, or ability to see past their noses. They're really like a bunch of animals down there. You remember, Kinsey."

"Yes, Sir. I remember," Kinsey replied.

"In your region, how many trainees did the Army accept?"

"I think it was eight, Sir."

"See? The General turned his head and looked down the length of table first to his right and then to his left where Wentworth sat among the other soldiers. "A whole town of people and only eight tested high enough to join our ranks."

"Yes, Sir," Kinsey replied.

Wentworth didn't know what to make of this. It was ridiculous for a General to pander to enlisted men in this fashion. Was Kinsey a part of this stupid performance or did he just get trapped in it by being in the wrong place at the wrong time?

"What's your name?" The General pointed a few seats down from his and across the table.

"Michaels, Sir."

"Where you from Michaels?"

"My town wasn't a named town, Sir," he answered.

"That's a shame. How many trainees came from your no-name town?"

"Two, Sir."

"We could do without you two if we had to, couldn't we?" the General asked the trainee.

The young man didn't know what to say.

"The Army would still be strong if the two of you weren't here." The General shoved more food into his mouth. "Right?"

"I suppose that's true, Sir." The trainee returned his eyes to his plate.

"Four eyes down there," the General spoke directly to Wentworth. His stomach clenched around the food he had just started putting in it.

"Yes, Sir," His reply sounded more composed than he felt.

"Would this Army be the same without you?"

Wentworth played along, "The Army is greater than the sum of its parts, Sir."

The General let his fork fall from his hand and crash into his plate, sending bits of food far from his tray.

"That is exactly what I mean. Well said, trainee. What's your name?"

A few heads turned his way as Wentworth answered, "Thomas, Sir. Billy Thomas."

Kinsey knew that he had assigned Thomas to watch over Wentworth and he reacted by slowly shifting his eyes to look at the trainee who was speaking. When he recognized Wentworth he nearly choked. Wentworth knew this was the moment of truth. Was Kinsey the General's lackey or was he the leader the Brothers were counting on him to be?

Kinsey's eyes got wide and he redirected the General's attention to himself. "That line is so good that I think you should send it out to every serviceman on the battleairship, Sir. It's inspiring."

"This ship could use some inspiration," the General agreed. "Men, it was good dining with you. I think I will do it more often," he announced, rising from his seat. He left his tray where it sat and strolled out of the Mess.

Kinsey leaned forward, "Thomas, may I speak with you in my office?"

"Yes, Sir," Wentworth looked longingly at the remaining food on his tray. He shoveled a few more forkfuls in, carried his tray to the return window, and followed Kinsey to his office.

When the door was closed, Kinsey threw his hands up in the air. "Are you crazy? Do you have a death wish? I've been playing a chess game with your life, moving you all around this ship to hide you, and you march into the Mess and start talking to the General?"

"It's been too quiet on the message boards. It's as if radio silence has been implemented."

Kinsey forgot his anger as he considered Wentworth's point. "Having the General show up in the Mess for the first time in my twelve years on the battleairship is another indication that something's wrong. He was campaigning." Kinsey shook his head.

"Are we ready? The order is coming soon," Wentworth said.

"We're ready," Kinsey assured him. "We'll halt any attack ordered for the Surface. The shuttlecraft will not leave the bay. Don't worry."

"Nothing that I'm witnessing is leading me to believe that I should not worry." Wentworth squeezed himself into Kinsey's locker where he had hidden before.

CHAPTER FIFTY-THREE

"Gerard, my old friend. It is good to see you!" Jonas embraced a man at least six inches taller than he was and looked to be at least ten years younger. The happiness the men felt to be in each other's company was tangible.

"I have been waiting for your call to action. All you have to do is say the word and your soldiers march!" Gerard said with a smile.

The two men studied each other for a minute. "You've become an old man . . . again!" Gerard said, making Jonas laugh. Mark, who looked on from his seat at the family table smiled to himself, while Lon, in the seat next to Mark's, looked confused.

"I've already stopped at the care center to see Ellie. Her spirit shines as brightly as ever," Gerard said.

"You'll meet our children at dinner. This is Mark Mead and Lon Walker." Jonas gestured toward the young men seated behind him. "They are the World Army defectors who have been helping to train our men," Jonas said.

"How many are with you?" Lon asked.

"We started out with one hundred. All are armed with at least one weapon. Some have more. We picked up some twenty or thirty men on the way. The wanderers are armed, but mostly with knives or metal pipes."

"What type of weapons do your men carry?" Mark asked.

Gerard reached into his long coat and handed Mark a gun. It looked like an M16 A6, which had been the World Army issue about seventy-five years before Mark's time. Mark had read about the history of the World Army in training and had taken interest in a time when the Army was able to issue weapons to every enlisted man. In the present day, the Army had whittled the defense budget and increased the Army's assets, requisitioning new battleairships and adding soldiers. Mark had a romantic notion about the old days when the Army guarded against invasions that never came—back when the purpose seemed clearer.

"This sure beats the six dilapidated guns that make up our entire weapons cache. How did you get this?" Lon inspected the weapon Mark had just handed him.

"That piece is so old, I'm not sure anyone knows exactly where it came from anymore. I heard that the original weapon was passed down twice before the great-grandson of the man who originally came across it decided to take it apart piece by piece. He had the idea to cast molds of the parts. He didn't have the luxury of experimentation, so he was deliberately successful in reproducing them. The ammunition took a lot longer to figure out, but once he did, our town began production of the weapons."

"You were caught!" Lon realized Gerard's town was the one he had been searching for on his quest to contact the battleairship.

"We were. Caught and punished by the World Army. We had the foresight to set up a decoy factory. We let them raid it and seize a share of our weapons. Then we set off to work again at the real production site. It takes a long time to find the right metals, melt them down and assemble one gun, but we've recovered most of what the Army took from us."

"Who turned you in and how did they contact the battleairship patrol?" Lon asked.

"Men will say and do things that are out of their character in times of duress. I don't have any interest in finding the guilty party or judging," Gerard said matter-of-factly.

Lon thought about how quickly he had divulged Mark's identity to General Hilgers and decided not to pursue the conversation any further.

"You must be exhausted." Jonas patted his friend on the back. "People in town have volunteered their homes and food for our new recruits. We haven't had a food drop in twelve days—since Mark and Lon came to visit," he joked. "But we will share what we have and still have plenty."

"Thank you, Jonas. We walked through the night and broke up into small groups, so men should be showing up steadily all day. I'm sure your townsfolk will pick out the strange faces right away."

"Everyone knows to send newcomers here first. I will disperse them to the right areas. After sunset, we will meet on the path in front of my house for training. You can count your men then and see how many made it."

"It's a noble mission we're on—they will be guided here safely," said Gerard.

"We have lookouts between your town and our border. We sent the children to play there all day. They will welcome your men while keeping watch for a possible Army attack by land," Jonas said.

"The attack is coming by air," Mark said confidently. He didn't say that his informant was a premonition.

"Still, the children can watch by day and the militia will watch at night. For now, you can rest here and we'll help your men get settled in as they arrive."

As if on cue, four men climbed the steps to Jonas's house. Jonas, Lon, and Mark made a list of who showed up and where they were sent to stay. Gerard slept easily and soundly throughout the remainder of the day despite the constant stream of men coming and going from the house.

Later that evening, Ellie served a jovial dinner where no one got enough to eat. Gerard marveled at Sarah and John and entertained the kids with stories of their father as a young man. Once the dinner had been cleared, the men descended the stairs of the home to greet the militia members gathering in the roadway in front of Jonas's home.

One hundred and twenty-seven newcomers had arrived that day. The men who had come with Gerard were a formidable group. They were united with the Dwellers of Jonas's town by circumstance and they were anxious to fight the World Army, but that common goal wasn't enough to unite them as an army of their own. The men from Gerard's town stood together in a large group beside the locals. The factions didn't mingle or make introductions. They stood in two defined units and looked at each other with guarded curiosity.

So that the large group could see him, Jonas addressed the crowd from the top stair of his home. He projected his voice as far as he possibly could, but men still had to repeat what he said for those in the back.

"Thank you for coming," Jonas began. "As you know, we have discovered that there is a WA base between our towns. We believe, based on what we have recently observed, that the conflict we expected with the Army may begin soon. Our towns, the most populated and sophisticated in our region, have been working together toward declaring our independence from the World Army. As you may have heard, residents of our town have been successful in creating a water purification system."

Cheers rose up from the newcomers in the front and then, seconds later, more cheers echoed from the back where the delivery of the news had been slightly delayed.

"We have also been getting ourselves in shape for the physical fight, if it should come to that. We are thankful to be joined by new recruits led by my trusted friend, Gerard, who have brought more than one hundred guns to aid us in our fight with the World Army. If they fire at us, we will be able to fire back."

After hearing about the weapons, the men from Jonas's town applauded and yelled with excitement.

Confident that he had shown each side of the divided group the attributes of the other, Jonas proceeded with that night's training exercises.

The men broke into smaller groups and rotated between calisthenics led by Jonas and Gerard and instruction with Mark and Lon. The young trainees were able to provide priceless details about the weaknesses of the WA shuttlecraft. Mark admired how naturally his counterpart took to being an educator. Lon was in his element in front of the men and his enthusiasm was contagious. He repeated the same information countless times that night, tirelessly reciting the important details.

"Each shuttle is equipped with a blaster. The craft cannot detonate the blaster until it has landed and transformed to a land vehicle. The kickback would cause the craft to crash if it attempted a blast in flight. Our best strategy is to make sure that the shuttlecraft does not land."

Lon explained that disabling the craft would be difficult, but not impossible. "The exterior electrical panels are the shuttle's weakness. We need to get men underneath the craft to shoot out the panels covering the electronics and avionics. We want to bring the craft down on our terms—heavily damaged and in a heap of metal." All of the men loved this part of the lesson. "Then we can gain access and deplane the crew. It isn't our intention to take lives. It is our goal to protect ourselves and to declare independence with as little collateral damage as possible, but they will be sending their best soldiers on this mission. We won't get a shuttle full of trainees like Mark and me—we'll get the hard core guys who have seen action, so be prepared to do whatever is necessary to keep yourselves and your families safe."

Mark quickly followed Lon's lead, learned his presentation, and gave a few of his own tutorials during the night. The young men had formed a strong bond and made a good team, but the one thing they couldn't agree on was the time of day that the Army was most likely to attack. Mark thought they would descend at night, hoping to catch the Dwellers off guard. Lon thought that the Army would disguise the mission as a much needed-food drop, drawing the Dwellers outside. Then, instead of food, they would deliver a decimating laser blast. They told the members of the militia to be vigilant day and night. The two trainees ended their lectures with the same words—*always be ready*.

When the training was finished, the men dispersed throughout the town to catch up on some sleep. The children were ordered to continue their watch the next day and the men would start watching the skies the following night.

Mark wished that she had told him *when* they were coming.

CHAPTER FIFTY-FOUR

The General chose to deploy his soldiers at 03:00. As much as he loved the crew's dramatic reaction to the sound of the Quartermaster's whistle, it wasn't necessary to call all hands. Walthers had hand selected a specialized unit to execute his covert operation. They were devoted officers whose years of service had groomed them to be killing machines. The General knew that giving the orders himself would convey the importance of the mission, so he began with the first name he had written on his list.

Major Blake Kinsey answered his video monitor with a bleary-eyed expression, but snapped to attention when he saw who was calling.

"You have an assignment, Major. Be in Launch Bay Seven in ten minutes for briefing." The General ended the communication and proceeded to the next officer on his list of six.

Seven minutes later, as the General walked onto the deck, a deep voice called, "Attention on deck!" The six crewmembers that had been called to duty, along with the soldiers who worked in bay, snapped to attention and saluted the General.

The General let the unit maintain their positions rather than allowing them to be "at ease."

"You are being deployed to the Surface to contain a weapon constructed by the Surface Dwellers. They have developed a system for filtering chemicals from natural elements. The by-product of this filter is used for the sole purpose of creating a weapon of mass destruction. This is a covert mission and no flight plan will be filed. The coordinates of your destination are in the nav. After you set down, you will convert the aircraft to a land vehicle and blast the nearest town until it is completely destroyed. Then, you will travel approximately 174 km to the West and level that domicile in the same manner. You will leave no survivors."

* * * *

Aboard the shuttlecraft, Kinsey chose the seat across from Bensen, the only other Brother on board. The two made eye contact and their wordless communication was understood. They hadn't anticipated these circumstances—the Brothers had been planning to halt a Surface strike before it was initiated, but Kinsey and Bensen liked their odds. Allowing the shuttlecraft to leave the bay was a very attractive alternative to the original plan. With only four other soldiers to overthrow, mutiny on board the shuttlecraft would be far easier to accomplish than overthrowing the entire crew of the battleairship.

"We have lift-off," the Captain said in a calm voice.

"Lift-off," the SIC confirmed.

The craft began to propel forward until they were clear of the bay.

"Clear." Kinsey and the rest of the crew could hear the pilots in their headsets.

"Clear."

"Gentlemen, we will descend ten thousand feet to reach our destination in five minutes. We will land the craft and Gunner Sanders will execute the order for the blast. Our orders are to leave no survivors and we will discharge our weapon until we have completed the mission. We will then proceed to our second target and discharge the blaster at that location. You will be back in your bunks within the hour. We will maintain radio silence until we reach our destination." The Captain unkeyed his mic.

Kinsey started the timer on his watch. He had four minutes and fifty-five seconds to figure out how he was going to sabotage the mission. And to communicate the plan to a man he couldn't speak to— the soldiers were silent in their concentration. Kinsey wondered if the men were mentally rehearsing their duties as they had been taught to do. The mission wasn't a difficult one and only half the crew had tasks to perform. The rest were just back-ups. Kinsey hoped that the silence came from the realization of what they would witness and what they would forever be responsible for if they carried out the General's orders. But, by the look on most faces, that wasn't the case. Kinsey could see that the men were excited by the order to exert deadly force. For these soldiers, this was the moment they trained for and the moment they had visualized many times. This was their chance to be woven into the fabric of the history of the World Army.

Kinsey worked out a plan and tried to allow for contingencies. He knew that the lives of many innocent people depended upon him getting this right. Thinking of them gave him the courage and resolve that he needed. He would get one attempt to save the Dwellers, and he was determined to come through.

CHAPTER FIFTY-FIVE

The sound was so foreign to life on the Surface that it instantly woke everyone who heard it. The reverberation of the pulse engines traveled for miles and cut through the complete silence that typically prevailed in the stillness of night.

In Jonas's house, the reaction was instantaneous. Mark, Lon, and Gerard had fallen asleep hunched over the table; but the second that the sound entered their consciousness, they shot to their feet.

"Ellie, stay inside with the children." Jonas kissed Ellie on the cheek and made his way for the door.

Gerard had supplied Jonas's house with two trench coats loaded with weapons—Nappy's coat, which held Humphries' weapon, hung on a peg next to the others near the front door. Each of the men grabbed their combat gear and put it on as they sprinted down the front steps. Men were flooding onto the paths of the town, looking overhead for the craft, yelling to their families to take cover, and coordinating with each other.

"Go to where we landed before!" Lon yelled to Mark. "I have a hunch." Lon had no way of knowing for sure, but he doubted that the crew would take the risk of setting the shuttle down on unfamiliar terrain at night.

"Go, go, go!" Mark and Lon sprinted to where the shuttlecraft had landed twelve days ago. The trainees covered the distance faster than the Dwellers who followed them. The shuttlecraft came into view as the pilot expertly lowered the craft to touchdown. The militia's training and plan of attack had focused on not allowing the Army to land. The craft's unchallenged arrival froze many of the Dwellers in their tracks. They weren't mentally prepared to execute the mission as planned and they certainly didn't feel confident about changing tactics at this juncture.

"We'll distract them!" Mark yelled to Lon as they continued towards the craft. "We can act like we're expecting them to rescue us. It'll give the militia the chance to attack if we can delay the discharge of the blaster."

"Affirmative!" Lon yelled from Mark's flank. As they reached the shuttlecraft, they slowed their pace and saw the craft turn on its spotlights. The glow of the lights illuminated the Surface area in a twenty-yard perimeter around the shuttle. Mark and Lon walked into the lit area and began to wave their arms wildly. As they did, the turret containing the blaster slowly turned until it was aimed directly at them. Seeing that the young trainees had become targets, the misfit militia was empowered by defiance and courage. They lined up behind their courageous leaders, but remained in the shadows.

Without facing the men behind him, Mark yelled loud enough to be heard above the engines, "Lon and I are going to act like we're expecting a rescue. We think that will distract them just enough to give you the chance to attack. If you want to save your families, we need to get aboard that shuttlecraft. The external door lever for the hatch is just forward of the door. It unlocks automatically upon landing. Split up. Group One, breach the craft through the hatch. Group Two get into the cockpit. There is an external access panel for the avionics bay just aft of the forward tread. Pop it open and climb through."

From behind him, Mark heard several voices confirm the order.

Inside the shuttlecraft, the crew caught sight of Mark and Lon. "Captain, there are two men approaching. One is wearing a Trainee uniform," The Gunner reported through his headset.

"I see them. Stand by," the Captain replied.

Kinsey and Bensen made eye contact as they tried to predict the ramifications of the latest development.

"It's Walker, Captain. I recognize him," the Gunner reported. "He and the man with him are indicating surrender."

"General Walthers, how would you like us to proceed?" The Captain radioed his superior officer who, he knew, had been monitoring communication aboard the shuttlecraft.

After twenty seconds, forever in military time, the Captain wondered if the General had copied their communication. He was considering calling again when the General responded with his order.

"Arrest the trainees and restrain them through any means necessary, Captain. Then proceed with your mission."

It was clear by looking at the men outside the craft, that the delayed reaction of the shuttle crew had made them extremely anxious. They searched the cockpit windows for movement and darted glances at the blaster to watch for a sign that it was engaged.

The Captain switched on the external P.A. speaker, allowing him to broadcast outside of the shuttlecraft.

"This is Captain Miller. I accept your surrender on behalf of the World Army. You are under arrest. Kneel down with your hands behind your heads. Lieutenants Norman and Gibbs are coming to get you. Do not resist."

Mark and Lon got down on their knees. They saw the cabin door lowering and two officers deplaning.

"They're makin' it easy!" one of the Dwellers remarked.

"Let them get all the way to us, then rush the craft. Lon and I will take care of the officers."

"Yes, sir!" A Dweller behind Mark shouted, sounding very much like a real soldier.

The two Lieutenants covered the twenty-yard distance quickly and were within a foot of Mark and Lon when the trainees sprang from their positions and tackled them, wrestling them to the ground.

"The trainees have engaged the soldiers," the Captain reported to the General.

"Fire at will, Captain." the General's reply was immediate this time.

"Yes, sir."

"Gunner, fire at will," the Captain ordered.

"But, Cap, our guys are still out there," the Gunner replied.

"Fire at will, soldier. That is an order!" the Captain yelled.

Kinsey and Bensen had been waiting for their moment. The Gunner's hesitation gave them the opportunity they were looking for. Kinsey tore the Gunner from the turret and Bensen delivered a right hook to the soldier sitting next to him.

The Captain turned toward the disturbance and was shocked to see a dirty man crawling through the avionics access panel into the cockpit.

"Fire that blaster, Gunner!" the Captain yelled as his eyes searched the empty turret for the Gunner.

A very solid object struck the Captain in the head just above his right ear. The impact snapped his head to the side and disoriented him momentarily as he tried to determine the source of the pain. His vision was a bit fuzzy, but it seemed that the dirty Dweller with the beard and the crazy smile was holding a slingshot.

Dean laughed out loud. "Got ya!" he shouted, placing another big rock in his sling.

"Watch your six!" The Captain shouted to the crewmembers in the main cabin—two more Dwellers were charging into the shuttlecraft.

"That's enough out of you. You need to go to sleep now," Dean said calmly as he smacked the pilot with another well-aimed rock. The strike hit the center of the "lights out" bulls-eye and the Captain collapsed over the yoke.

Bensen and Kinsey incapacitated the Gunner and the other soldier. They tied their hands and feet together and laid them face down on the deck of the shuttlecraft.

Dean fired one good shot at Bensen and the other two Dwellers had attacked Kinsey before they were able to convince the militia that they were the "good guys."

Kinsey addressed the Second-In-Command who had remained in the right seat in the cockpit. "Has that blaster been engaged?"

"I don't know," the SIC said too inanely to be lying.

"That's not an answer, soldier. Has that blaster been engaged?" He repeated slowly, his volume increasing with every word.

Mark and Lon boarded the shuttlecraft, ready for more action, but found only heated conversation occurring as they assessed the scene. They were followed by four Dwellers carrying two listless lieutenants who had received quite a beating—a thumping fueled by the anger that comes from decades of deprivation.

Mark eyed Kinsey—he needed help conquering the giant man. The soldier beside him didn't look like an easy target either.

"They's the good guys!" Dean said in response to the concern on Mark's face.

"I'm Major Kinsey and this is Sergeant Bensen. Wentworth is going to be very happy to see you," the Major addressed Mark.

The Gunner started laughing from his position on the floor. "Before you start planning reunions, you ladies might want to close the cabin door. When the blaster goes off we'll have Surface dust polluting the air and the blowback from incinerating that worthless town will make it impossible for us to breathe."

Mark looked from Kinsey to Bensen. "The blaster is engaged?" He asked, filled with panic thinking about Jonas's family.

"I can't get a straight answer out of these assholes," Kinsey said kicking the Gunner in the gut with the toe of his boot.

"I just told you it was engaged," the Gunner coughed.

With a small gesture of his hand, Mark signaled to the four Dwellers nearest the hatch to go warn their loved ones.

"How do I disarm it?" Kinsey demanded.

"You'll have to kill me, Kinsey. I have a direct order from the General and as long as I'm alive, I'll carry it out." The Gunner tried to sound tough, but he could barely get enough air to whisper his valiant speech.

"You questioned your order just two minutes ago!" Kinsey shouted down at the Gunner. "You better get your alliances straight."

Kinsey moved briskly to the cockpit where the Captain was still slumped over the shuttle's yoke. He placed his arms under the Captain's armpits and dragged him to the back of the craft where the other soldiers were tied up.

"Make sure that he won't be a problem when he wakes up," Kinsey ordered Dean.

"Yes, Sir!" Dean executed a perfect salute and did as he was told.

"You guys want to go on a plane ride?" Kinsey asked Dean and the other two Dwellers who remained aboard the shuttlecraft.

"Absolutely!" Dean answered for everyone.

Kinsey then addressed the SIC, "Turn off the radio and take us up. We're not in a hurry."

The junior pilot wasn't going to be a hero. He saw that the Captain was still unresponsive and bleeding from two separate head wounds. The Dwellers scared him more than he would ever admit. He had seen desperate men commit unthinkable acts when he lived on the Surface and now the Major had taken to assaulting his fellow officers. The SIC decided instantaneously that his allegiance was to himself and that he would do whatever was necessary to get out of this mess unscathed.

"Yes, Sir," the Second-In-Command replied to Kinsey's order.

Mark looked out the window of the shuttlecraft. He hoped that this would not be the last time he would see the town that he had so quickly adopted as his home. To his surprise, no one had fled to take cover at the news of the blaster being engaged. The army of Dwellers stood at the ready to protect and defend themselves until the end. Mark searched for Jonas among the large militia. As the ship prepared for take-off, the Dwellers realized that the World Army was retreating and they began celebrating by cheering, waving their fists, and embracing each other. The spontaneous celebration made Jonas easier to find—he was the only one not showing outward signs of relief and jubilation. He stood near the front of the crowd, with an arm outstretched toward the shuttlecraft as if offering a prayer or sending positive energy to the crew—to Mark. The sight of the Knower gave him renewed resolve and, with it, a sense of peace. Mark sent love and energy back to Jonas, his family, and to the town. He took his seat and buckled in for the flight back to the battleairship.

"Set a heading for the battleairship and let me know when we are within range of their guns. Engage the weapons detection radar and put up our shield." Kinsey barked orders to the one-man flight crew.

The SIC had turned a sickly gray-green color. "Do you expect that we will be fired upon, Major?" He asked.

"Be ready," Kinsey commanded.

He left the aviator to sweat by himself in the cockpit and joined the others in the back. He was satisfied with phase one of his on-the-fly plan. Mark's and Lon's contributions had certainly made it easier to thwart the attack on the Dwellers.

Kinsey sat in the seat next to Mark and across from Lon before buckling himself in. "Bensen will brief you on what you've missed aboard the battleairship. Welcome to the Brothers of the Rebellion, boys."

Kinsey began formulating a plan for phase two.

CHAPTER FIFTY-SIX

"Captain, er, Major Kinsey, we are a mile from Battleairship Two-Zero." The Second-In-Command reported the position of the shuttlecraft to his new superior officer.

"Hold the pattern," Kinsey told him. "And turn on the radio."

The SIC flipped a switch. "Done, Sir."

Kinsey grabbed the Captain's headset and pressed the mic key. "General Walthers, this is Major Kinsey, over."

Mark, Lon, and Bensen grabbed headsets and listened to the radio conversation.

"Major, what the hell is going on down there? The craft has not responded to any of our communications, over."

"General, we've managed to bring everyone back alive, but we need assistance. We request that you open the bay door and send a team of medics to meet us. We are repositioning to dock the craft and I will be on the Bridge for debriefing in a few minutes, Sir."

"Negative. Major. Your assignment has not been completed. You are not authorized to terminate the mission," the General replied.

"The mission had to be aborted, Sir. We encountered hostility on the Surface and several crewmembers sustained serious injuries. The Captain, Gunner, and two lieutenants need immediate medical attention, but we were able to arrest the two A.W.O.L. trainees as you ordered, Sir." Kinsey held Mark's gaze as he spoke with the General.

The radio was silent for a full minute.

The four men waiting for the General's reply grew edgy. Mark and Bensen looked out through the craft portholes to make sure that the battleairship had not turned its guns on them. The Major seemed to be breathing heavily and Lon cleared his throat repetitively and unnecessarily. Finally, when the transmission came, the General spoke softly and deliberately, fully conveying the depth of his fury.

"Army Police will meet your shuttle. Walker will be taken to the Brig and Mead will be brought to me. You can get your men to Sick Bay before you report to my office for debriefing. Your failure will cost you, Major."

"Yes, Sir. Major Kinsey out." Kinsey and the others removed their headsets and the Major addressed the SIC, "Turn the radio off."

"The minute we land, AP are going to be all over your asses!" The Captain yelled from the floor, spitting the blood that still cascaded down his face from his broken nose.

Dean calmly removed his soiled, tattered scarf and gently tied it around the pilot's mouth as a gag.

Every set of eyes on the craft was on Kinsey, waiting for what came next.

"The General is sending APs to get Mark and Lon. Lon, they're going to try to take you to the Brig. I'm going to have Bensen go with you. You have to pass the laundry on the way. When you get near the laundry entrance, I want you two to take down the AP's and to yell for the Brother's of the Rebellion to help you. Once you're free, find Wentworth--he's hiding out in the laundry--tell him to order the Quartermaster to signal General Quarters. Then bring as many Brothers as you can and make your way to the Bridge. The General wants me to take the injured soldiers to Sick Bay, but I'm going to let someone else handle the garbage. I'll be the highest-ranking officer in the landing dock, so I will delegate. You men stick with me," Kinsey instructed the Dwellers. "You'll be a great distraction. The Army Police and the soldiers have never had guests like you aboard before."

"Aye-Aye, Sir!" Dean yelled enthusiastically.

Kinsey looked out the porthole. "Take your seats, men. Buckle up. We may be in for a rough landing." He referred to the fact that the SIC, a less experienced pilot than the Captain, was at the controls.

"This might be a good time to give you the message I have from Jonas," Dean whispered to Mark as they buckled into seats next to each other. "He says you owe him a favor. He told me to beg you not to risk your soul. Increase your faith. Remember who you are, no matter what happens up here."

Mark pictured Jonas's strong, calm gaze and could almost feel his reassuring hand. Mark thought back to a few days ago when Jonas said that he might call on him to do something difficult. It wasn't surprising that Jonas's request was one that did not benefit him personally.

Mark took a deep breath. "I'll remember that all of this is just part of a Journey—not true reality at all."

Dean nodded his head. "Stay away from the shadows," he advised.

"Docking," the flying pilot called out as he was trained to do, even though there was not a second crewmember in the cockpit to echo him.

As the SIC set the craft down, Kinsey reiterated the plan to Mark. "We have men in every area of the battleairship. They are waiting for the signal to mutiny. When they hear the Quartermaster's whistle, they will begin securing their areas and then descend on the Bridge. You'll get back-up. Don't try to take the General down alone. Every soldier on this ship was trained to give his life for the commanding officer. There are still some who won't hesitate to kill you if they think he's in danger." Kinsey shook Mark's hand. "Good luck. We'll be coming, just hang in there."

Kinsey turned to address the men who had been bound on the floor and the newly acquired Brothers, "The trainees will deplane first, escorted by the Army Police. We want it to look like the General's orders are being followed. Once they're away from the shuttle, we will deplane. Walker and Bensen, get that pipe blown as soon as possible. Until that alarm sounds, we will be fatally outnumbered. After it blows we will just be ridiculously outnumbered, so squawk the signal on the double."

Kinsey removed the Captain's gag.

"New plan, Kinsey. Thirty seconds after we open that door, you're going down."

"That mouth of yours is why you are going out last," Kinsey told him.

"Lower the main hatch door," Kinsey ordered the SIC.

Six Army Police soldiers were already waiting. Four stepped forward to the bottom of the plank. The one in front held out a pair of handcuffs. "Trainee Mead, you're coming with us."

"All you guys just for me?" Mark quipped as he deplaned. "It's not like I have super powers or anything."

"Shut up, Mead. I don't think you'll be in the mood for jokes once you're standing in front of the General."

Mark smirked and held his hands out in front of him.

Kinsey stood behind the young trainee in the doorway of the shuttle. He recognized one Brother among the four young AP's who were taking charge of Mark. "He won't run; there's nowhere to go. You don't need to restrain him."

The AP who was poised to cuff Mark looked at Kinsey disbelievingly, but he didn't dare to question the Major's order. "Yes, Sir."

Kinsey addressed the remaining APs. "You two take Walker to the Brig. He doesn't need to be cuffed either. Sergeant Bensen will supervise as you escort the prisoner."

"See you soon, man." Mark smiled at Lon and gave him a single, sure nod.

"Really soon, Brother," Lon assured him as the APs steered him toward the Brig.

"Walk, Mead." One of the APs pushed him. "You know the way."

Mark led the APs into the ship, past the Mess, and down the passageway where his quarters were located. Mark amused himself by imagining what the ship would look like through the eyes of the tourist Dwellers. He was sure that they had never seen such gleaming surfaces, such advanced technology, or such abundant supplies of hot food. Even if the mutiny failed and they were relegated to the Brig while the General decided what to do with them, they would be overwhelmed with the luxury of their accommodations.

As the APs escorted Mark to the Bridge, he remembered how recently he had been there to get chewed out by the General. He wondered if he would get reprimanded again for having a beard, or if that would seem like a meaningless infraction this time considering Mark's recent advance to calculated mutiny.

The General's assistant was not at his desk because it was the middle of the night. The APs knocked on the General's office door and were met with a short command.

"Come in."

The General sat behind his desk in full dress uniform. He smiled at the sight of Mark in custody.

"Why isn't he restrained?" the General asked.

"Major Kinsey told us it wouldn't be necessary," one of the soldiers said nervously.

"He wasn't a problem, Sir," added another.

"Dismissed," the General told the APs, never taking his eyes off of Mark.

The young men left the room and closed the door behind them.

"Welcome home," the General began.

"Yes, Sir. Walker and I were shocked when our fellow trainees threw us from the shuttlecraft. We didn't know what to think when the craft didn't return to rescue us. It was then, Sir, when I realized that you could not possibly be aware of the truth behind what happened to us. In that vein, I think you must not know the living conditions of the Surface Dwellers, or you would lobby the World Army on their behalf for more assistance." Mark appealed to the General's huge ego to buy some time.

"What is it that you think I don't know, Mead?" The General asked. "Do you think that I don't know that you switched places with Wentworth to escape the battleairship?"

Mark hoped that the speech would continue, giving the Quartermaster time to sound the alarm.

"Do you think I don't know that the Surface Dwellers have inadequate supplies of food and water and that the food often contains deadly bacteria and synthetic hormones guaranteed to control the population in such a gradual way that the connection between the food and the dying wouldn't be noticed by the simple-minded Dwellers?"

Mark didn't reply.

"Do you think that I don't know that the idiot Dwellers have manufactured a filtration facility? Do you think I don't monitor their radio communications? Do you think I don't know about our World Army base on the Surface or that General Hilgers ordered Walker's execution?"

The General was just hitting his stride.

"Yes, Mark Mead. This Army is aware of all the aforementioned. You haven't earned the right to be informed yet, but you were selected to be one of the few men that would understand that all of these seemingly horrible things are necessary so that only the fittest of beings can survive. You would have come to understand that in time. Does that surprise you?"

Mark's only response was to breathe in, then out, and repeat the pattern.

"Betcha I know a lot of other stuff that you don't know I know," The General teased. "I know that your favorite word is *shit*. I am aware that you changed your name to the name you were given on Tier Three. I also know that you shadowed recently."

Mark's next breath was a gasp.

The General was very satisfied by the baffled expression on Mark's face.

"Did you meet anyone interesting on your last shadowing trip?" The General's eyes challenged Mark to answer his question. "Did you learn anything new?"

Mark's stomach fell. "Marcus?"

The General laughed. "I told you I've taken on a slightly more intimidating form."

"Didn't you ever wonder how *you* were chosen as a trainee for the World Army? Your grades were not exceptional. In fact, you are not exceptional in any way. Yet you were chosen to become one of the elite. You never questioned why that was?"

Mark's head was spinning.

"It's because I got here first. I got ready for you. You see, I had the advantage of meeting a woman who told me that our unfinished business would bring us together again, *Dad*," The General said sarcastically. "This time I wanted to have the upper hand. I wanted to be in control. Isn't this perfect? I am in absolute control over what happens to you!" The General leaned back in his chair.

"Marcus, you blame me for what happened. I understand that. I've tried to explain that your perception is wrong. You were very young --,"

"Shut up. It doesn't matter what happened then. What matters is what's happening now."

"It don't care what you do to me," Mark said. "But you're endangering your soul. Your hate for me has overshadowed your Journeys and you have allowed yourself to jeopardize your own Enlightenment. I can't stand by while you throw away the soul that your mother and I created and, whether you believe it or not, would lose our own to save."

"I said SHUT UP!" The General shouted. "You're not in charge here. I am. You're in my world now. I control everything that happens to you. I'm not going kill you, Mead. I have men to do that."

"Your moral obligation extends farther than your own hand," Mark shouted back. He regained his composure. "And so does mine. Which is why I can't allow you to continue on this Path."

The General laughed. "You feel so invested, don't you? I guess that's because you don't have all of the information. I told you already--I made a deal to save myself and my mother from the darkness."

The piercing squeal of the Quartermaster's pipe filled the room, building the pressure to an intensity that was difficult to endure. The sound was followed by the Quartermaster's voice, "General Quarters, General Quarters, General Quarters, this is not a drill."

A scuffle erupted outside the General's office and, while Mark turned his head to see if the fight was coming through the door, the General reached into his desk and pulled out a handgun.

"You're not the only one who doesn't care what happens to you, Mead. I guess I'm weak because I just can't deny myself the pleasure of doing this. You're leaving the Tier, Dad. I wish that I could eliminate you from existing all together, but I've learned that a being can never *not be*, unfortunately. At least my mother will be safe from your inadequate and persistent love for this lifetime." The General's face exploded into a genuine smile. "The funny thing is, after all your searching and shadowing to find her, you're finally in the same place at the same time. She's aboard this ship right now. Ironic isn't it?" The smile turned to a sneer. "Too bad you can't stay."

The General pointed his weapon at Mark and fired.

CHAPTER FIFTY-SEVEN

Six Brothers were fending off soldiers on the stairs leading to the Bridge. The fight was confined to hand-to-hand combat, so the unexpected sound of a gunshot got everyone's attention as it bounced off of every hard surface of the battleairship. The recognizable but uncommon sound temporarily paused the action and then intensified the fight.

"Shots fired!" Lon screamed to Bensen and the other Brothers who had rushed the Bridge. The two APs who stood guard outside the General's office were contained quickly, but soldiers came in waves to defend the Bridge and their leader.

Dean and the other Dwellers had followed Kinsey's directions and arrived on the scene just in time. They sidestepped the brawlers, and climbed the stairs to where Lon and Bensen were in command of the General's outer office.

"Watch them!" Lon shouted to Dean, pointing at the APs who were tied to office chairs.

"We're going in," Lon announced to Bensen and the Brother AP. "Watch my six and rush the General. Mark wasn't armed, so Walthers is the shooter."

The door to the General's office was not reinforced. Lon expected a steel hatchway, but it was a flimsy office door made of particleboard. Lon was thankful for the General's arrogance as he lowered his shoulder and easily burst through to the other side.

Mark lay on the floor and the General stood over him with his back to the entryway. He was yelling about how he wasn't going to let Mark die quickly. At the sound of the door crashing in, the General turned towards the disruption.

Lon was the first to reach him. He propelled the weight of his body against the General, but his smaller frame only made enough impact to throw the General off balance. Bensen went for the General's right hand, which held the weapon. He was able to apply enough pressure inside the General's wrist to get him to release the gun.

It hit the ground with a thud and Mark quickly recovered it. Together, the two trainees and Bensen wrestled the General to the floor, rolled him onto his stomach and tied his hands behind his back with a zip tie.

"Get his feet," Lon instructed.

The General was incapacitated. He and Mark had reversed positions and Mark was now the one standing over his prisoner.

"Where is she?" He demanded.

The General spit at his feet.

"Tell me where she is," Mark repeated.

"Or what? You'll kill me? You're too worried about your precious soul to harm anyone. She's safer with me than with you anyway," the General said.

Major Kinsey interrupted the interrogation by broadcasting on the ship's Public Address system.

"All crewmembers, this is Major Blake Kinsey. The General has been detained by Army Police. He is being arrested for military crimes as we speak. The World Army has relieved him of his duties and has placed me in command of the ship. I order you to cease and desist in fighting among yourselves. The ship is on lock-down. Return to your quarters until further notice. Failure to comply with this order will result in arrest and court-martial. Stand by for further communications." Kinsey ended his announcement.

Mark knew that the message was loaded with half-truths, but he hoped that it would calm the infighting.

"Hear that?" Mark asked the General. "This isn't your ship anymore. Do what's right. Tell me where she is."

"If you love her so much, follow your heart," the General taunted.

Mark could see that further conversation was pointless. He turned to Lon, "Thanks for coming."

"Told you I would." Lon looked at Mark's left arm, bleeding through his dirty coat. "You okay?"

"Yeah. I've got more important things to worry about now than a gunshot wound."

Mark walked into the outer office and was happy to see Dean there.

"I need you to come with me," Mark told him. Dean was at Mark's side before Mark ever offered an explanation. "She's here. The one I shadowed for is here and I need to find her."

"Let's find her, then!" Dean's smile raised his beard two inches.

Mark centered himself for a minute and tried to guide himself to where she was in a manner similar to how he shadowed using her as the destination.

The battleairship was huge and pockets of fighting made it hard to navigate the passageways. The obvious place for her to be was in the General's personal quarters, but Mark wasn't being pulled there. He followed his instinct and descended into the lower decks of the ship. He ran to the office of the Army Police with Dean at his side.

When they got there, the door was closed and when Mark tried the handle, he found it locked. It was an airtight door and there was no way of breaking through it.

"You're sure?" Dean asked, pointing to the door.

"Yeah, this is it."

Dean reached into an inside pocket of his coat and removed the heavy metal slingshot. He clanged it against the door repeatedly.

"We need an AP out here right now! The deck is being taken over by Surface Dwellers!" Dean screamed at the top of his lungs.

After about five minutes of incessant banging and yelling, the door opened inward.

Mark and Dean threw themselves against it, causing the heavy door to swing in with such force that it sent the AP behind it to the floor.

Two more APs crouched behind their weapons in the rear of the room forming an armed human barrier in front of another closed door.

"Freeze!" One shouted.

"I'm Mark Mead," Mark raised his hands. Dean raised his too, but still held the weapon, so it looked like an attack posture. The AP's pointed their guns at Dean in tandem.

"Put it down," Mark calmly reminded him.

"Oh, yeah," Dean smiled and let the solid piece of metal slip from his hand. It made a deafening clatter as it hit the steel floor.

"Did you hear the announcement?" Mark asked the APs.

"That was bogus," the younger one replied.

"It's not. I'm with Kinsey. I'm one of the trainees that was thrown out of the shuttle and left on the Surface. The General is not in command of the ship, Kinsey is. He sent me for the girl. I can take you to him to verify the order," Mark told the APs.

"Who's that?" The older AP gestured towards Dean.

"He's with Kinsey too," Mark told the AP. "He's from the Surface where all this started."

"I have direct orders from the General to keep her safe. Until I hear differently from him, she isn't leaving here."

Mark and Dean looked at each other. They had definitely found her.

A fight broke out in the passageway, close to the AP office door.

"We just need to see her," Mark pleaded. "We won't try to take her out of this room."

The APs weren't convinced.

The shouting in the hallway came closer.

"Stand down, soldier. Major Kinsey is in charge of this ship and we're under lock-down. Go to your quarters or you're under arrest!" The commanding voice carried from the passageway and reached the APs office.

"You heard that," Mark said to the APs. "I'm telling you the truth."

"We're not leaving," the younger AP told Mark.

"Don't. Stay right here. Just open that door and let us in."

"It's open." The older AP lowered his weapon and stepped aside.

The younger one looked at him incredulously.

"I don't wanna get court-martialed," he explained.

Mark opened the door and found her inside the room, cowering on the farthest side of a small cot that looked out of place in the office. She was covering her face with her arms.

"Hey," he said gently.

She recognized his voice and looked up. A hopeful smile appeared beneath her red, swollen eyes and tear-stained cheeks.

"It's you!" she whispered, only half believing her eyes.

"It's me. And you're gonna be okay. I promise. I'm here now," Mark told her.

"Where's Marcus?" she asked.

"He's fine, I just saw him. He told me where I could find you." Mark tried to set her fears at ease.

"I don't know where I am, Mark. Or why I'm here. But if I'm with you, I must be home." She started to cry again.

Mark sat next to her on the cot and took her in his arms. He stroked her hair as she buried her face in his chest.

"Shhh, baby. It's okay," he reassured her.

Mark couldn't stand how shattered she seemed. She was fragile, scared, and unsure. He knew that this wasn't her true nature. The Knowers had been right. He had found her where she was supposed to be—recovering in peace on Tier Four.

"Can we leave this place?" she asked him as if she were able to read his mind. "Can you take me to where you live? Please protect me, Mark."

"I'm going to make sure you're okay," he promised. He held her for a long minute and then called out softly, "Dean?"

Dean poked his head in the room.

"I need you to help me shadow her—I've never attached to a soul before. I don't know how to do it."

"It won't work unless she is your true soul's companion. You aren't a shadow right now, you're a full being," Dean warned.

"We're one," Mark assured him.

"If anything happens to your being while your shadow is gone--," Dean shook his head.

The fighting in the hallway had escalated. Both sides were benefitting from reinforcements.

"I know. That's why we have to do this now," Mark said firmly.

"Okay, surround her with love and let her soul fill the space in yours. You'll take her into yourself and you will fit into her space. Like two

240

halves making a whole. You'll feel it when the connection is complete. You can't set your course for her as a destination, so you'll have to have a good idea where you're going."

"I've been there before," Mark told him.

"Keep the image of the place in your mind," Dean told him.

"Marina always pulls me back," Mark told him. "But I don't know if I'm coming back this time."

"You can't be a complete soul without your being. It is a huge risk to stay out of your being for an extended time. I know. I've done it, but there are many who haven't been as lucky as me." Dean didn't want to tell Mark what to do, but he wanted him to consider what he was gambling.

"Stay here in case I need you—protect my being while I'm gone?" Mark asked.

"As best I can," Dean promised.

She heard the exchange, but concentrated fully on the beautiful reality of being in his arms again. She could smell his familiar fragrance, could feel the curve of his arms, just the perfect length to wrap her close to him. She could feel his chest vibrate when he spoke and reveled in the sound of his deep, smooth voice. She tried to breathe him in more with each breath. Resting her cheek against his skin, she nestled close to him in an effort to melt into him.

Mark knew what he had to do, but he hoped that he would be strong enough to execute the plan once he was faced with the deed.

He loved her completely. He tried to heal her through his unending affection, ease her worries, and fill her spirit with joy. He wanted to be the one to nurse her soul back to health. He wanted to stay like this, holding her and protecting her until she was ready to stand next to him again.

The love effortlessly formed the connection and propelled them to Tier Four.

CHAPTER FIFTY-EIGHT

She looked around at the soft, rolling hills. The vibrant green color was a shockingly beautiful contrast to the gray world that Marcus had taken her to visit. Her eyes squinted involuntarily at the golden glow of the sunlight. She breathed the sweet air deeply and lifted her chin to allow the soft breeze to caress her face.

"Isn't it beautiful here?" She turned to face Mark

Tears streamed down his face. "Yes. This is a magical place. A healing place," he agreed.

"From the time I arrived here, I felt your love surrounding me," she told him. "I knew it was you and then you finally came." She gently kissed his lips.

"Never doubt that my love for you is endless. It's timeless and nothing will ever change that," Mark said through his tears.

"Why don't you tell me that every day then, just to make sure I don't forget?" she suggested playfully.

"You're going to have to remember," he said, choking up.

"Mark, you're not leaving me, are you? You said you would protect me," her face reflected her worry.

"This is where you belong right now," Mark told her gently.

"I belong with you, so you're staying here too. Aren't you?"

Mark held her close and starting crying in intermittent, explosive bursts. He wanted to stay—tried to think it through. If she left this Tier and went to the Transition Tier, he could just send his shadow back to his being . . . unless something happened to his being, making it impossible for his soul to be whole again.

The thought of Marcus crept into his mind. He would need to be contained so that he didn't try to abduct her again. Marcus wanted revenge on Mark and Mark needed to give him the chance to claim it. He needed to act as bait to keep Marcus away from her. Mark was sure that Marcus's hate for him was stronger than his love for his mother. Given the choice, Mark knew that the immature soul would prefer to pursue him.

There was no way that he could justify defying the Plan.

"We are together. Even when we are not in the same place at the same time, our souls are attached. You said that you felt me here before I arrived, right?" He lifted her chin to look into her eyes.

"Yes."

"Then you know that what I say is true. We are together always. And we will be in the same place together when the time is right."

"You're leaving me here!" The realization sounded like an accusation.

"Do you trust me?" Mark asked her.

"More than I trust myself," she told him.

"I'm doing what is right and what is best for both of us," he assured her.

"Can you come to me like you did before, so that I know you're real?" Her eyes pleaded with him.

"I don't think so," Mark told her. "It's hard to explain, but--,"

"It isn't approved?" she guessed.

"Yeah. That's exactly right."

They stood close together looking into each other's eyes, quickly blinking the tears away as they blurred their sight. They inhaled their sniffles and took deep breaths to stifle sobs.

"Protect Marcus," she said softly.

"I will."

Mark tried to hold her gaze, but his vision was split with the viewpoint of his being.

Dean fought wildly with two APs while Mark's being wrestled on the floor with another one. The heavy metal slingshot was just beyond Mark's reach and the AP who was on top of him lunged to retrieve it. Mark's left arm ached relentlessly--the gun wound was rendering it nearly useless. He wouldn't be able to defend himself against a blow from the weapon.

On every other occasion when Mark had shadowed, large chunks of time passed on Tier Six while he spent what felt like a few minutes with her. Now time was showing how abstract and indefinable it was. Mark could see that the minutes were ticking off at the same rate in both locations.

Mark heard Dean's voice calling him back.

"I have to go now. For us to be together again, I have to go now," he told her.

"I love you," she pressed her lips to his.

Mark could see that the AP had the thick piece of metal in his hand and was poised to smash it down into Mark's skull.

Mark put his hand on the back of her head and gently pulled her mouth deeper into his own.

"I love you too," he said, closing his eyes. If he saw her standing in front of him, he would never have had the strength to leave.

CHAPTER FIFTY-NINE

Dean's kick made contact with the APs arm. The blow didn't knock the weapon to the floor as Dean had hoped it would, but it delayed the strike that was on the way to Mark's head.

The two APs who were struggling to control the Dweller were having a hard time hanging on to him because he was difficult to grip inside his long trench coat. Dean remained squirrely—he had no formal combat training, but his unconventional methods were effective.

Out of the corner of his eye, Dean saw Mark's right fist make solid contact with the AP on top of him.

"Welcome back, kid!" Dean yelled.

Mark turned his heartache to rage and quickly had the upper hand against the AP. It didn't matter that his left arm was shattered or that he weighed fifty pounds less than the guy on top of him. Mark tossed him to the floor as if he were an empty uniform. Mark used his right forearm to press against the APs throat.

"Are we done here, or do you want me to finish this?" He yelled in the APs face.

The AP managed to nod. Mark reacted to the surrender very slowly, letting the military cop know that his windpipe only remained intact at Mark's discretion. When Mark got up, the AP stayed on the floor. His hands flew to his neck, and he began coughing.

Mark grabbed the bigger of the two APs trying to contain Dean and swept him off of his feet. He landed on the floor with a thud, involuntarily expelling the air from his lungs. After a kick to the midsection, he'd had enough. The AP threw his hands up and blinked repeatedly to get his eyes to focus.

Dean picked up a wooden desk chair and smacked the last vertical AP with it, sending him to the floor in a groaning heap.

"Yes!" Dean cheered himself and looked around to see if Mark needed backup. He smiled at the mounds of incapacitated APs that littered the floor. "Boy was I glad to see you! You came back just in time." Dean noticed that there was a large amount of blood splattered on the floor. He eyed Mark's left hand, which was covered and dripping. "Come 'ere. I'm gonna fix you up."

Dean tore a strip of fabric from his tattered trench coat and made a tourniquet above Mark's bleeding wound.

"I can't have my best employee bleedin' all over the place," he said as he worked.

"Dean, I . . ." Mark searched for the right words.

"I know, kid. I know," Dean said. He finished tying off the fabric and slapped Mark on his good arm. "Let's go see if we can take down more of these Army boys. I know little girls on the Surface who fight better than them. It's kind of fun kicking these young guys' asses."

The twosome made their way toward the Bridge. It was easier to walk through the passageways now. The fighting had been contained to small skirmishes that probably had little to do with the mutiny. Mark knew what happened when young men got heated up—they looked for something to hit.

At the bottom of the stairs leading to the Bridge, Mark and Dean were stopped by newly placed security.

"I'm gonna need your ID," said a soldier who Mark thought smelled like the laundry room.

Mark reached into his pocket and took out his military ID—his real one—and remembered Jonas's advice to keep it in case he needed it in the future.

"Mead?" The young soldier's eyebrows raised and he nodded approvingly. "Welcome back, man."

"Thanks. He's with me." Mark gestured to where Dean stood behind him.

"You're both free to pass. I think there are some faces up there that you might recognize."

Soldiers from the Brothers of the Rebellion blocked the stairwell and the entrance to the Bridge, so Mark had to clear a path. He used his deep commanding voice to get the GIs to get out of the way, "Make a hole! Make a hole!"

The outer office was filled with loud conversations as soldiers of all ranks worked together to carry out the procedures they had planned before taking control of the battleairship. The first face Mark that focused on looked a lot like his own—on a good day.

"I'm back from vacation, Went, but I didn't bring you anything," Mark announced.

Wentworth looked up from the tablet he was holding and handed it to one of the trainees who had been standing next to him. He made his way to where Mark stood.

"I thought I'd never see you again," Wentworth said through a wide smile.

Mark laughed at his friend's fatalistic disposition.

"I figured I probably got you in some trouble, so I had to come back to make sure you didn't take my heat," Mark explained.

Wentworth nodded his head. "Yeah, well you started some shit," he said, using a word he had learned from Mark.

"Kinsey told me everything you did."

"Nothing more than what you do for your brother," Wentworth said.

"Aren't you gonna hug him?" Dean asked loudly from behind the reunion.

Mark and Wentworth slapped backs and Mark flinched at the pain in his left arm.

"You're hurt?"

"Little bit," Mark admitted.

"It's your lucky day--the medics are on our side. I'll take you to Sick Bay," Wentworth offered.

"After I talk to the General," Mark promised.

"He's in there." Wentworth pointed to the General's office door where Kinsey stood guard outside.

"How is he?" Mark asked as he approached Kinsey.

"Just the way you left him," Kinsey replied.

"Give me a minute alone with him," Mark requested as he entered the office.

The soul of the boy he loved with his entire being was lying on the floor trapped inside the vessel of a large, hate-filled Army General. The sight of him hog-tied and disabled hurt Mark's spirit.

"There's still plenty of time for you Marcus," Mark began.

The General's feet faced Mark and he didn't make any effort to turn to look at him.

"You found her?" He guessed.

"She's safe," Mark confirmed.

"No one is safe with you!" the General yelled.

"I don't know how to make you to see the truth. If you could see it, you wouldn't have to carry the heavy burden of the lie that you believe. Buying into that lie has changed everything about you, Marcus. Your natural spirit is a loving, joyous one. This state you're in now is part of the lie. This isn't you," Mark said softly.

"You have no idea who I am. Your phony caring doesn't work on me--I'm not as naïve as she is," the General told him.

"She's worried about you too."

"She should be worried about YOU!" The General rolled to his side, revealing that he had freed his hands from the zip-ties. It took him less than a second to draw the weapon from inside his jacket and fire a round at Mark's chest.

"See you around, Dad," the General said through bared teeth as he emptied the cartridge into Mark's being.

CHAPTER SIXTY

Mark awoke to the familiar fragrance of orange blossoms. He was aware of the love that surrounded him. He was overwhelmed to be receiving so much love—to have so much feeling pouring into him. The Spirit of Love was at his side. He was home.

Mark hadn't planned on being back here so quickly. He hadn't even spent twenty years on Tier Six. He typically lasted much longer than that.

The Spirit of Love gave Mark the opportunity to exercise his free will. "Would you like to retain your memories of Tier Six? You are not rewarded or penalized for collecting memories and your soul will have the benefit of your experiences whether you are aware of those memories or not. You will graduate to higher frequencies, regardless of your awareness to do so."

"Yeah," Mark said wearily. "But I have a confession. Something that I don't want on my soul," He tried to look at The Spirit of Love in spite of his unworthiness to do so.

"Speak your mind, free your heart," The Spirit encouraged him.

"I shadowed. I was told that it isn't sanctioned, but I did it anyway to see her."

"I know," The Spirit answered without any hint of judgment.

"I'm heartily sorry," Mark told The Spirit.

"I know that as well," The Spirit answered.

"Can I still Journey or will there be a setback?" Mark asked.

"You may Journey forward," The Spirit told him.

"Thank you."

"Would you like to appeal now?" The Spirit asked Mark.

"No," Mark answered simply.

"Are you ready to progress to Tier Seven, or would you like to stay here and rest a while?"

"I'm ready," Mark smiled at the thought of what may be ahead of him.

CHAPTER SIXTY-ONE

Mark's awareness increased with every Journey, allowing him to connect with his memories of former Journeys at earlier and earlier ages. Mark had been looking for her since his ninth year on Tier Seven. Seven years would seem like a lifetime to most sixteen year-old boys, but Mark had a larger perspective.

Tier Seven was pleasant enough. He had been born to a family consisting of two hard-working parents and three older sisters. Mark's arrival gave the family the little prince that they had been hoping for.

Mark's sister Ellie, was his favorite. He recognized her early on and he always felt happy in her company. Ellie shared his love for the ocean and taught him to swim before he could walk. Ellie worked as a sailing instructor every summer and had arranged for Mark to get a job at the sailing school this year as well.

Mark's first class of students was made up of five kids ranging in age from eight to fourteen. There was only one girl's name on his list. It was a name that Mark had adored for several lifetimes.

The morning of the first class, Mark woke up early and went for a run. As the supposed sun materialized on the horizon, Mark was starting his sixth mile. Mile seven led him home where he enjoyed a long, hot shower and carefully inspected his freshly cut hair. He was a bit younger than she had ever seen him before, but he hoped that he looked much better than when she had last seen him. He had been covered with Surface grime and randomly grown out facial hair, not to mention his bleeding, shattered arm.

Mark was the first to arrive in the family kitchen and he whipped up a hot breakfast for everyone—his famous favorite, shrimp and grits. Ellie woke early to help him. She knew that he would be incredibly excited today and she was eager to witness the reunion that had been three lifetimes in the making.

"Are you nervous?" She asked him as they sat on the sailboat deck, watching the students get dropped off one by one.

"Only that something will prevent her from coming," Mark answered. He looked tan and handsome in his crisp white polo shirt emblazoned with the sailing school logo and his khaki cargo shorts. He bounced his right knee a hundred times per minute, as the time to begin the class got closer.

Finally, when he didn't think he could endure another second, an older model convertible pulled up in front of the sailing school. A smiling father dropped off his raven-haired daughter. With a kiss and hug, he sent her to learn a new school skill and, hopefully, make some friends who shared her enthusiasm for the water.

Mark called to her without making a sound. She looked around and surveyed the landscape before her eyes settled on him. He stood up and smiled a smile that had been waiting far too long for this moment. His heart beat in frantic, ecstatic rhythms that would have been hard to dance to.

She walked slowly towards the boat as he leaped from the deck onto the dock to greet her. She held her hand out to him and he took hold of it. The small gesture restored their part of the Universe.

"I'm Mark Mead," he said, replaying the scene as it had been on the first day they had met on Tier Three.

"Nice to meet you, Mark Mead. I'm Dahlia Wade."

Mark's smile threatened to split his face in two.

He was captivated by the presence of her.

Ellie's panicked gasp broke the spell and Mark looked up. Out of the corner of his eye, he saw the shadow advance and then retreat as quickly as it had appeared.

THE END ... AND THE BEGINNING

From the Author

Thank you for taking the time to read Tier Six. I hope that you enjoyed the Journey as much as I enjoyed the process of creating it. If you wouldn't mind helping to spread the word about the book, your reviews and recommendations are greatly appreciated! Social media can give #TierSix a life of its own!

Many thanks to my beta readers; Patrick J., Rita B., and Sharon G.! Your feedback and encouragement are invaluable.

Thank you Gary G. and Kelly B. for answering my military and aviation questions. I'm sure I should have asked more.

Love and respect to my oh-so-meticulous copyeditor Sharon G. (Did I need another (.) after that last (.)? See how much I need you?) Any mistakes that remain in this work are MINE, not hers.

Connect with me on Twitter: @MarciGiebels
Email: Marci@MarcisVoice.com
Look for the Tier Six Novel page on Facebook

Also by Marci Giebels

The Francis Kelly Project

Eighteen years after The Francis Kelly Project disbands, an A-List Hollywood actor hears their demo and decides that one of the songs is the perfect title track for his new film. A nationwide search is conducted to find the cutting-edge newcomers. A country obsessed with American Idol style contests stands by waiting to meet the up-and-coming group of musicians. Will the forty-somethings reignite a forgotten dream and win over an industry that values youth more than talent? Or has their big break come too late?

Coming Soon From Misty Morn Publishing:

Beneath The Sand

Henry's Lucky Underpants

Dreams Are Memories That Haven't Happened Yet